KNIGHT
HEARTS

Michael watched the slugs bounce away harmlessly where they should have perforated the radiator. The truck was armour-plated.

KITT continued dumping smoke into the air until the place looked like a riot zone. *Smoke,* thought Michael – *smoke fouls lasers.* If the boys in the truck were toting American 180s, their sophisticated targeting system was in trouble. Laser beams could not spot targets through smoke, and apparently KITT had anticipated this.

Bullets ripped the snack table apart one *hors d'oeuvre* at a time. Seeing nowhere to run, Trini Ortiz dived into the fountain as holes dug their way across the concrete rim where he had been sitting with his wife Donna.

A lower chuddering noise, a .30-calibre gun perhaps, suddenly cut through the machine gunfire, and Michael watched the remnants of the tiered white wedding cake explode like a sapling hit by a buzzsaw.

KNIGHT RIDER III: HEARTS OF STONE

Glen A. Larson and Roger Hill

Based on the Universal Television Series
'Knight Rider'

Created and written by Glen A. Larson

A TARGET BOOK
published by
the Paperback Division of
W.H. ALLEN & Co. PLC

A Target Book
Published in 1984
by the Paperback Division of
W.H. Allen & Co. PLC
44 Hill Street, London W1X 8LB

First published in the United States of America by
Pinnacle Books, Inc., 1984

Copyright © MCA Publishing, a Division of
MCA Communications, Inc., 1984

Typeset by Phoenix Photosetting, Chatham
Printed and bound in Great Britain by
Cox & Wyman Ltd., Reading

ISBN 0 426 19705 4

FOR
STEVE CHRISTIAN
who knows my secret

1

Michael Knight had not been inside the confines of a church since he was nine years old, and this particular church struck him as quite intimidating.

The nave seemed a mile long, with a wide aisle separating row upon row of pews, their perfect geometry reaching to the carpeted steps which formed the apex. The dark mahogany of the pews gleamed in the dim light, polished to a high sheen by generations of churchgoers sliding in and out of them, buffing the wood with their Sunday best. Michael self-consciously glanced at his own blue jeans, pullover, and black leather jacket and felt a tiny stab of embarrassment, like an unwanted flashback from a naughty childhood. Then he felt briefly stupid for feeling embarrassed. The church was definitely making him uncomfortable, as it seemed designed to do.

He stepped out of the dimness of the vestibule. The sunlight outside was heavily filtered by the thickness of the east wall's stained glass windows. The complex pictures depicting Biblical scenes toned the light down and threw it in multicoloured shafts across the nave.

Gilt winked down at him from the vaulted recesses of the roof of the nave. There were gargoyles up there, watching, and Biblical characters, styled after Michelangelo, staring at the visitors to the church with sour countenances.

Michael cranked his head back even further, and saw the clerestories above, admitting more tinted light. Vertebrae crackled in his neck. He was dogtired, having just made the New Orleans-to-San Antonio drive in one jump with KITT and having been diverted to the Houston metro area en route by a radiophone call from Devon Miles.

The sleek Knight Industries Two Thousand was parked in front of the church, the Texas sun warming its flawless black alloy hide, and Devon was sitting in his well-appointed office at the Foundation for Law and Government in west Los Angeles, sucking up air conditioning and maybe a tumbler of iced tea. And Michael was stuck with the church. It had taken him forty-five minutes to find once he'd got off the freeway, even with KITT's sophisticated map display terminal and scrupulous directions. Eight blocks south from his present location, the neighbourhood became a bona fide barrio area; the church was in the mostly well-to-do buffer zone between that and the downtown area of Houston. The collection-plate business at this particular branch of the Good Lord's house had been very gratifying indeed.

Michael kneaded the stiffness out of his neck by working it with one hand as his attention turned to the choir lofts – there were two – above the pulpit area. Beyond them to the east and west were smaller vaulted chambers. Viewed from above, the floor plan of the church would undoubtedly be seen as a classic cross, a quirk of architecture common to many older houses of worship, the ones that predated the split-level suburban structures that were their West Coast cousins.

The carpeting gave the huge, hollow building a tomblike quiet. Ahead of Michael, placing votive candles and murmuring prayers, were several people – a black man, in farm clothes, holding a battered straw hat to his breast in supplication; several older women shrouded in black,

2

mourners, perhaps, for some departed relative, conversing in Spanish and weeping discreetly; a younger woman, also Hispanic Catholic, dressed in a simple summer frock and scuffed shoes. Her skin was a perfect coffee colour, her eyes were as black as coal chips, or black diamonds, and her rich fall of dark hair reached nearly to the backs of her knees. She was also – as Michael saw when she stood up – nearly seven months pregnant.

Michael looked from the woman to the gold and silver of the elaborate communion plate as he approached the altar. The poor labourers and common folk he saw before him did not pay for the opulence of this place, though a large chunk of their collective incomes was certainly destined for its upkeep.

A priest in full church uniform of surplice and stole glided past behind Michael like a wraith, vanishing through a small oaken door off one arm of the huge cross shape.

Michael felt terrible. He was supposed to be reporting back from a brief vacation, a little 'R and R' for the hard-working freelance hero-type, he thought, to wash the taste of the Liberty Cox affair out of his mouth.

Liberty Cox had been an investigative reporter and had uncovered the lovely truth that a cable television mogul was actively sabotaging a charity event called the Alternative Energy Road Competition. She had fancied herself enough of a journalistic hotshot to convince the mogul she could blow the whole thing wide open; the mogul had responded in a not unsurprising manner by kidnapping her, planning to button her up until the race was done and then dump her in the nearest reservoir wearing a concrete necklace. She had also messed up Michael's undercover assignment, which was to ferret out the perpetrators of the sabotage, and he wound up having to practically break his neck and many speed records to save her lovely face from becoming so much hamburger.

In the midst of danger, they had traded smart remarks to blow off steam and were ultimately attracted to each other. She had an acerbic personality and a fabulous physique and had invited Michael to New Orleans for a bit of time off.

3

Michael had accepted, much to Devon's chagrin, and at first things had been just rosy.

They started to grate on each other by the third day. With typical reporter's zeal, she began to grill him about Knight Industries. There were uncomfortable questions abruptly posed during odd, even intimate moments – particularly about the nature of Michael's association with the corporate empire of the late tycoon Wilton Knight. What *exactly* was his job, as she kept putting it, maddeningly.

Michael gradually got the idea that Liberty was more interested in an exclusive byline topping an exposé on the Knight monolith (as she saw it) than would ever be in him or his life. His leavetaking was quick, but not without pain.

You think you would have learned by now, he chided himself, still watching the young pregnant woman.

His rest-and-relaxation trip an utter washout, Michael piloted KITT cross-country to their California nest, and then the call had come in from Devon.

Michael's mentor – he never thought of the tall, urbane, distinguished Devon as a 'superior' – was either in one of his impenetrably moody intellectual funks . . . or he was purposely not telling Michael everything over the radiophone. Something hot regarding the flourishing trade in illegal arms shipments to Central America was in the offing, but Devon had been annoyingly vague on details. He instructed Michael to proceed to Houston and contact someone in the church who would reveal the name of what was presumed to be a vital contact in the gun-running chain. That was it. Once that was done, he was to 'await further instructions.' Devon cut him off on the radio; it was a tactic Michael normally enjoyed employing when Devon's enquiries got too distracting during moments of danger or stress inside KITT. Michael discovered that he *hated* the shoe being on the other foot, and that had been another bad page in a whole encyclopedia of recent personal depression.

Even KITT wasn't talking to him much lately. Or was that just his fertile imagination, running away with him? He thought of the song, 'Imagination.' Behind its catchy rhythms, the lyrics told the story of a guy going bananas from an inability to distinguish between delusions and fact.

Now he was feeling sorry for himself. He blamed the oppressive atmosphere of the church.

Liberty Cox had been a pain – and the whole aftermath of the affair had become a pain in Michael's neck, back, and behind. He needed to take some sort of psychic aspirin to wash it all away, replace it with something else . . . and out of the blue had come Devon with his cryptic mission.

Come to think of it, if Devon wanted Michael to stay put in Houston, he was probably en route himself, either in the Knight 2000 jet or the Foundation semi – KITT's mobile garage and tune-up facility – that Bonnie Barstow had dubbed *Rook One* for radio reference. Bonnie was a capable diagnostic technician, an able woman with degrees in robotics and computer science and a nose for pinpointing malfunctions and repair potentials in KITT's ever-changing equipment configurations. She was constantly putting into operation the improvements in KITT devised by the technical staff at the Knight estate in Nevada.

And, Michael smiled to himself, she was pleasing to the eye and ear (Bonnie's esoteric education had left her with a cultured accent that made her rather the female echo of Devon – though in Bonnie's case it appealed to Michael instead of making him feel under the scrutiny of an 'old school' British headmaster). The tall and competent brunette made an admirable fourth quarter to the team of Devon, KITT, and Michael and, as with most people Michael had admired or trusted in his life, they had got off on entirely the wrong foot on the occasion of their first meeting.

He visualized Bonnie piloting the big Knight trailer truck; probably rendezvousing with Devon at the airport. Then would come the patient-pending Devon surprise – most likely a job for Michael and KITT that needed to be done yesterday for some bureaucratic reason. The team was perpetually on the verge of being *too late* and having *not a moment to lose*, or worse, *no time to spare*. Michael grinned privately. If Devon had any pet phrases, they were probably all florid ways of saying *hurry up*.

So if Devon was always in such a rush, why the mystery, why the delays?

Michael shucked his jacket and draped it over one forearm. Tugging back the cuff on his shirt sleeve, he keyed on his wrist comlink, the watch-sized device that put him in instant contact with KITT, outside.

'You still there, old buddy?' he said in a low voice. Nobody in the church noticed.

'*It seems unlikely that I'll be anywhere else until you come out, Michael,*' responded KITT in the strange Boston twang programmed into his vox-box unit, courtesy of the psychologists at Knight Industries. '*I have been occupying myself by calculating the total number of bricks used in the construction of the building's west wall, by determining the average number of bricks in the most representative horizontal row, and multiplying –*'

'Okay, okay,' said Michael. 'So you're bored stiff; I'm just stiff. I'll be out in a minute, just cool your muffler, huh?'

'*Take your time, Michael,*' came the disembodied mechanical voice through the tiny speaker vent in the watch face. '*Mr Devon wishes me to inform you that he is on his way here to explain the situation to you more fully.*'

'Nice of him.'

'*He did not even give me any more details,*' KITT added, sounding somewhat taken aback.

'May I help you?'

The sudden intrusion of the voice caused Michael to snap his head guiltily up. His sore neck protested. A priest was standing in front of him, regarding the whole scene with a quizzical expression on his face.

The blinker on Michael's watch face – which strobed red whenever KITT was speaking – winked out. Michael felt abandoned.

The priest was nearly middle-aged but stocky and stout, kindly in the manner of most priests, handsome in broad strokes rather than in delicate facial brushwork. He did not appear aged, except for his eyes, which were also a contradiction. To Michael they radiated that open frankness affected by the Irish, but clearly this priest was of one hundred percent Hispanic descent, although his inflection did not hint at his background. He was as comfortable speaking English as Mexican dialect and exuded the confidence on which his ability was based. A strong man, Michael thought, a good man.

'Er, yes,' Michael said, ignoring the fact he had just been speaking to his wristwatch, 'I wonder if you could tell me where Father Carlos Laguna is?'

The priest smiled and rolled his eyes. 'Ah – Father Laguna, is it? Are you sure you wish to speak with him? He is always late; never on time. Some people suspect the depth of his faith but who knows?' He shrugged. 'Deeply religious men often run contrary to stereotypes, yes?'

'I have to speak to Father Laguna.'

'Then look no farther – I am Father Carlos.' He slapped Michael's bicep with a broad hand. 'I'm sorry, it's just that you look so *lost*. Please forgive my little joke.'

'You knew me but I didn't know you,' Michael said. 'Now we're even.'

Something about Father Laguna's jolly demeanor was not right. Michael recognized that the priest had been carefully considering what he might say on the occasion of this meeting; his banter sounded rehearsed.

Father Carlos was looking at him; looking for something in Michael's eyes. He said, 'Then you are Michael Knight?' as a matter of form, but that was not what interested him.

Michael nodded.

'You were sent by this Mister Devon . . . ah – '

'Miles.'

'Devon Miles, yes,' said Father Carlos.

Michael got the impression that someone had just asked for his ID card. 'Devon mentioned that you were having some kind of special trouble,' he said, not really sure, but hoping to draw the priest out to fill in holes in the narrative he so far did not compute.

'Thank you so much for coming. We are embarrassed, somewhat, that we were compelled to seek help outside the

7

family.'

'The Lagunas?'

'Yes. What are left of us. Last Tuesday, at three in the afternoon, the *bandidos* shot and killed my brother Miguel. In the middle of South Houston. He was putting gasoline into his car, and they came for him, and they used automatic weapons. Miguel was dead before the paramedics could answer the phone.'

Now Michael was looking nervously around the church. People continued on their small religious missions as the pair talked quietly in the centre of the nave.

'Sounds like you need the police,' said Michael. 'Who put you in touch with Devon?'

'Devon Miles is known to us for reasons that involve your organization,' said Father Carlos, who was beginning to sould like a touchy secret agent in an Italian spy movie. 'The same reasons that disallow the involvement of the police. The attack on Miguel . . . the other attacks and shootings and raids . . . have all been hit-and-run. The police? They arrive forty-five minutes late, they question witnesses to get differing and useless accounts of what happened. They count the bullet holes. And then they return to their lives.' He held up his hands, palms open and empty. 'And Miguel is still dead. So we are not interested in the police.'

'You mentioned automatic weapons.'

At the words, the priest glanced around skittishly. 'Innocent people might have been killed. This is no longer a simple difference of opinion between the Lagunas and the *Corazones de Piedras*. This is a war. And we are dying.'

Something rang falsely to Michael. What was Father Carlos talking about – terrorism directed towards a family connected to the biggest Catholic church in town? No, the priest had said a war, and that meant two more or less equally armed sides. The Laguna family was more involved than Father Carlos wanted to let on, at least now. If it was a war, then the Lagunas did more than just play the victims.

Devon. Devon had the answers, Michael thought. His

questions were growing harsher inside his head.

'I haven't had a chance to talk to Devon yet,' Michael said, still sounding neutral.

'I must meet with a man following the one o'clock mass,' said Father Carlos. 'He will have for me the name of a contact who is an inlet for the weapons trade your Mr Miles no doubt mentioned.'

'He mentioned illegal arms shipments into Central America,' said Michael.

'Following mass I shall go directly to my sister's wedding reception,' Father Carlos continued, ignoring Michael's remark. 'I should like for you to meet me there.'

'And you'll pass along the name of the contact?'

'Exactly. And your Mr Miles will know how to instruct you once you have it.'

'Where is the reception?' Michael hoped KITT was picking all this up, surreptitiously over the comlink . . . and that gave him an idea. Casually, he checked the time and pressed a tiny silver stud near the comlink's wristband. The watch peeped once.

'Do you know where the Del Rio Ballroom is?'

Michael grinned. 'If I can find this church – even though I was late – I can find anything in Houston.'

Father Carlos gave him brief directions: what lights to look for, where to hang a right. It was not far from the church.

'I'll see you at the reception, then, just mention my name. I'll make sure the people at the door know yours.'

'That'll be fine, Father,' Michael said. 'I'll find myself something cool to drink, in the meanwhile.'

'Oh? You're not staying for mass?'

The innocence of the question caught Michael off guard, but he smiled his way out. It was time for his little gambit. 'I'm more interested in what connection a priest has to an illegal arms ring than I am in doing stations of the cross . . . *Father* Carlos.'

Father Carlos stiffened at that remark, but he returned a smile Michael felt sure was slightly phony. 'May the Lord be with you until this afternoon,' he said curtly.

'Sure thing,' said Michael, extending his hand. Father Car¹os's handshake was powerful and lasted exactly three pumps. Then he turned and bustled off toward the pulpit. Singers in gowns were beginning to mill around up in one of the choir lofts, and more people had shown up to place candles.

Michael rushed outside and around the church to where KITT was parked. He jumped into the pilot's bucket seat and immediately asked. 'Well? Did you get a reading?'

'*Yes, Michael,*' came KITT's voice. The gradated readout on the steering column – the vox-box – flashed up and down as the car spoke. '*Check your Number Two video monitor for the results.*'

The TV screen farthest to the right on KITT's sophisticated Super Dash blurred on. A yellow graph superimposed itself on the screen, and then a sequence of dancing, jagged lines bisected the graph for the exact duration of Father Carlos's handshake. The graph trends were projected, based on logical patterns, to give more of a readout to analyze – according to the digital box at the top of the screen, the handshake had only lasted for 2.7 seconds.

The graph showed heartbeat, blood pressure, and respiration, 'Spell it out for me, KITT,' said Michael.

'*The man was extremely agitated,*' said KITT smoothly.

'I could tell that. But was he lying, or was there something he left out, or was he just running scared, or what?'

'*Based on my brief reading, Father Carlos was telling you the truth, but selectively. Omission of facts is not necessarily lying. I would base his agitation on the two most probable factors – his uncertainty regarding your identity and his concern that the other people inside the church not overhear you.*'

'You got that from one handshake?' Michael said, amazed.

'*Not all of it. I "read" his tone of voice as well. He is obviously both afraid and angry – I suspect he thought you might be one of those –*' `

'*Corazones de Piedras?* Yeah. How's your Spanish, KITT? Speak any?'

10

'*Mas o menos,*' the machine returned. Michael often wondered who programmed in the decidedly strange sense of humour, and remembered the microprocessor circuitry that formed the essence of KITT's 'mind' and 'personality' were keyed to respond and develop by learning from the driver. In an odd way, KITT's sense of humour *was* Michael's; more precisely, they both sprang in different directions from the same root.

'Enough to translate?' said Michael.

KITT was silent for a moment.

'I'll give you a hint,' Michael urged. 'The first word means –'

'*I'll freely admit that my language banks are neither comprehensive nor up to date,*' said KITT. '*It is Bonnie's job to prepare me in accordance with the specific requirements of each mission, and we haven't checked in with the Foundation semi yet.*'

'Don't worry, we'll have you speaking like a native in no time,' said Michael. He switched off the vital signs readout he had signalled KITT to pull from Father Carlos via the comlink and Michael's well-timed handshake. He knew what he wanted to know, for now.

Michael pulled KITT out into the Houston traffic. He waited for a delicious moment before announcing to the car at large, 'Hearts of Stone.'

'*I beg your pardon, Michael?*'

'The *Corazones de Piedras.*'

'I see. The meaning has no meaning, apparently.'

'I think Devon'll be able to clarify it for you,' said Michael as he drove KITT along in the manual mode. 'As for me, I've got some questions I want to ask him about automatic weapons.'

2

Michael saw the shapely form of Bonnie Barstow, clad in her usual tight white service jumper, climb down from the cab of the Knight Industries service semi as he pulled up. She waved. Michael always wondered whether she was waving at him or at KITT – she seemed at times to be in love with the sohisticated black street machine.

He unfolded himself from the car – his neck was killing him, by now – and gave a salutatory wave of his own.

Bonnie sauntered over, hands sunk in the zippered pockets of her jumper. 'The prince arrives,' she said, pleasantly. Behind her the silver box of the semi gleamed in the hot noontime sun, giving off shimmering waves of heat.

'Uh-huh,' said Michael. 'If I'm the prince, where's the King? I'm requesting an audience. I've got a bone to pick over with him – I think.'

'In yonder trailer, kind sir,' Bonnie said. 'If you'll just kindly haul your steed over there up into the box, I'm sure you'll find King Devon sulking on his throne.'

Michael tossed his arms wide, in mock-Shakespearian fashion, playing along with the jest: 'Nay, kind lady, the drawbridge is not yet down! You would dispatch me toward certain death!'

Bonnie laughed.

'I presume you picked Devon up at the municipal airport,' Michael added.

'Right. And he's uptight about something, don't ask me what.' She turned to go back to the truck and lower the hydraulic lift so KITT could be driven up the ramp and into the box for servicing.

Bonnie's mass of rich brunette hair swung around behind her as she turned, and Michael enjoyed watching her walk back to the truck. 'Hey!' he called. 'No hello kiss?'

Halfway back she stopped, turned, and threw him a wink. 'Hang in there, Romeo,' she said.

Feeling like a man who has just missed his plane to Hawaii, Michael got back into KITT. 'You know, old buddy,' he mused at the car's dashboard. 'I never thought you'd end up as my rival.'

'*Bonnie has extremely good taste,*' said KITT.

'Thanks a lot. You drive yourself up the ramp, smart guy.'

The flashbar on the steering column clicked over to AUTO MODE. While Michael sat there with his arms folded, the wheel manoeuvred itself and KITT rolled up the trailer ramp without human assistance.

During times like this, after his *pro forma* sparring with Bonnie and his now-easy acceptance of the supertechnology that allowed KITT to drive himself (*him*, Michael thought – even I think of it as a sentient creature and not a machine), Michael frequently found himself reflecting on how weird his life had got, and how fast.

Several months ago he had never heard of Knight Industries, except when they made headlines, was not smitten in a distant but admiring way for anybody named Bonnie Barstow, had never heard KITT's prosthetic machine voice, and had no idea who Devon Miles – by now the key human being in his life – might have been. By every calendar except the one incorporated into the watch portion of his comlink, those few months were a million years of

14

difference. Not so long ago (forever, in retrospect) he had been a police detective, Lieutenant Michael Arther Long, attached to the Reno division of the Nevada law enforcement authorities. In his time he had worked Vice, Bunco, and Robbery. His brief stint in Homicide was by choice. Due to his intelligence adventures in Indochina, which included penetration of Viet Cong 'sensitives' under deep cover and a fling in a North Vietnamese prison camp undergoing hallucinations caused by a severe head injury, he was eventually drawn to participate in high-level 'sting' activities designed to snare criminals of the 'gold collar' class. He proved to be born for such chases, and racked up an impressive series of busts . . . but at the disturbing cost of many loyal and expert partners. And then a sting hadn't gone so well. Michael lost another partner – his best, Ralph 'Muntzy' Muntz, a guy nearly twice his age and all cop – and almost got put six feet under himself. Skill and talent had nothing to do with the fact Michael had survived a point-blank gunshot in the fact. It was a steel plate, a souvenir of his Viet Nam misadventures, that had deflected the slug, mutilated his face, and caused his entire life to change in one brilliant orange explosion.

Then Knight Industries interceded, saving his life, changing his face, giving him – however inadvertently – an opportunity to avenge both himself and Muntzy. The peculiar world-view of an old patriarch like Wilton Knight appealed to Michael, and when the old man died, Michael thought that the continuation of Knight's work was a small price to pay for his own life. There were other considerations, of course, including qualms about totally abandoning his 'old' life, but what it boiled down to was the transformation of Michael Long, suitcoat cop, to Michael Knight, the manufactured scion of the Wilton Knight dream. Michael had taken on Knight Industries' vast resources, its greatest technological inventions, the Knight name, and even a fair duplicate of the young Wilton Knight's own face, all to the end of helping those who could not help themselves against the gold-collar class of thieves and murderers. As corny as it sounded, that was the basic truth, but once you got past that you ran headfirst into the glaring fact that, in his short association with the Knight conglomerate's FLAG program, administered by the indefatigable Devon Miles, he had saved more lives and squashed more crime than in most of his police career. It might have *sounded* Lone Rangerish, but by damn, thought Michael, it sure seemed to *work*, to slice past befuddling bureaucracy and get things down on a practical level, neatly turning the legal loopholes used by the upper criminal classes into nooses with which to hang them.

So why was Devon bothering to intercede in what was gradually coming to appear, to Michael, as a gang war between two groups of gunrunners, *both* of whom were illegal to the teeth?

Michael's hair-trigger anger was being aroused.

'*I suggest that you calm down a bit before you speak to Mr Devon,*' said KITT.

'What?' Michael looked down to the Number One video monitor and saw his own vital signs readout. KITT had scanned him.

'*Breathe deeply,*' the car advised.

'Right.' Michael self-consciously exhaled a few puffs and then climbed out.

Beyond the bay of the semi, specifically designed (in large measure, by Bonnie Barstow) to accommodate KITT, was an office/leisure area patterned after the Foundation office in Los Angeles and its various branches. There were several leather flared swivel loungers and a compact kitchen across from the computers, monitor systems, and other mechanical paraphernalia needed to maintain KITT.

In the centre chair, Devon swivelled to see Michael getting out of the car. His fingertips were joined together in a steeple, as always when he was thinking. Devon was rarely more than two feet from a phone, and one such panel telephone with coded buttons was built into the drop table at Devon's right elbow.

He looks like the head of SPECTRE, Michael thought.

Devon stood to his imposing six-foot-two height and the creases in his sharp, three-piece suit obligingly smoothed out. Devon would walk about in the Texan heat in that constricting, overly formal getup without raising so much as a bead of sweat, Michael knew. In many ways he was very impressed by this paternal, proper, silver-haired gentleman, the hub around which all of Knight Industries now turned . . . but to admit it would be horribly improper. Especially to admit it to Devon – it would supply the older man with leverage that he would wield over Michael, sometimes seriously – the father-son syndrome – or with his strange personal brand of humour.

'You've met with Father Carlos, I presume?'

'Oh, I met with him, alright. Only now I need you to tell me what all this subterfuge is about, Devon old boy.'

A pained expression constricted Devon's face. 'Please, Michael, not –'

'Old boy?' said Michael, wearing an imp's grin.

'Yes. I apologize for being so mysterious on the radio, but there were events and data I had to verify before proceeding.'

They both grabbed nearby walls to balance themselves as the semi lurched into motion on the highway.

'I don't know where to start to try and explain,' said Devon, looking a hair uncomfortable. Michael noticed that his silver hair was a bit wild at the temples, as though he'd slacked off on his strict grooming regimen or not gotten much sleep. That put them on a more equal footing, thought Michael, who still felt wrung out and weary.

'Perhaps this is best,' said Devon, moving to a cabinet set flush into one of the work consoles on the far side of the trailer box. From it he gingerly lifted a stubby machine gun Michael had seen only once before in his life. 'Do you know what this is?'

'Yeah – cops used to call it the Buck Rogers gun,' Michael remembered. The memory did not stretch that far back, perhaps a year.

'More properly, this weapon's designation is the "American 180,"' said Devon, holding it by the strap and passing it to Michael. 'Already in use by an estimated three hundred police and military organizations. Something that

17

would have been the stuff of cheap science fiction pulps a decade ago – a laser-sighted automatic rifle.'

Michael tested the gun in his grip. It was surprisingly light.

'The weapon incorporates a battery-operated helium-neon laser mounted under the barrel as a sighting device. It projects a dot of red light on which the bullets home in. Very useful for picking off a target in a crowd without killing or wounding everyone in sight.'

'I remember the test I saw of this thing,' Michael said. 'They scragged a dummy in a car with it at fifty feet.'

'It can perforate wood, concrete, car doors . . .' said Devon. 'Its other statistics are equally impressive – or frightening.'

'Depending on which side you're on.'

'Yes. For example, it empties a 177-round clip in five seconds, for a fire rate of 2,150 rounds per minute. It takes longer to *change* the clip than to empty it.'

Michael whistled, awed.

'Its accuracy – the "hit rate" – tests fifty percent higher than any other rifle ever tested. As you can feel, it's lightweight. It's also recoilless.'

Michael could tell from the heft of the gun that it was loaded.

'Ever fire one?' said Devon.

'Uh, no.'

He thumbed down an intercom switch. 'Bonnie pull us over for a bit, will you?'

Bonnie's voice filtered through the speaker. 'Done,' she said, and the truck slowed.

Devon pushed open the access doorway in the side of the trailer, and metal steps unfurled to road level. They were alone on the desert highway.

'Fire at that dead cactus over there,' he indicated.

Michael saw the cactus, a saguaro, black with rot and drooping in the sun like an ugly scarecrow. No harm in wiping this one out – that sort of thing was against the law in the desert states.

As Michael held the gun. Devon reached across and

pushed a safety-like toggle on the grip. Michael swung the gun to port. Even squinting in the blazing sun, he could see the quarter-sized red dot whip across the surface of the cactus, then back. Without even looking down at the gun – although the urge to sight came automatically – he squeezed the trigger gently.

The Buck Rogers gun cut loose an eight-round burst before his brain could signal his trigger finger to ease up. The cactus came apart in the middle in a spray of vegetable rot, as though hit by a helicopter blade, its upper half tumbling backward and plopping onto the scrub.

The first salvo had taken Michael by surprise. He put his teeth together and scanned the red dot a foot down from his first target area. He fired again, this time blowing away a perfect horizontal slice of dead cactus, which spun away into the air. Then he fired vertically, and the remainder of the cactus sprang open like a banana peel without a banana.

Devon stood, arms folded, waiting for an opinion.

'Makes an M-16 feel like a slingshot,' Michael said, watching smoke curl out of the barrel. The American 180 ate .22-calibre ammunition, but that only made it sound misleadingly small league. Five such shells into a highly concentrated area were more damaging than a single heavier-calibre bullet, and the laser made sure the bullets went where they could do the most damage.

Then things started to become relevant to Michael. 'Is this what the Lagunas are running into Central America?' he asked, gesturing unconsciously with the gun.

'Not exactly,' said Devon. 'I mean to say, that isn't the problem with the Lagunas.'

'So be my friend, Devon. Give.'

'Our concern is a kind of modern-day range war, a conflict over territory and markets.'

'Between the Lagunas and the *Corazones de Piedras?*'

Devon nodded. 'Known in Anglo circles as the Stones.'

Michael bit his lip. He had heard of a group called the Stones in Viet Nam – and not the Rolling Stones, either. They were rumoured to be a renegade phalange of Rangers and Green Berets, guys missing in action or presumed dead, who holed up in the jungles and fought the Cong their own way – raiding supply dumps on both sides for provisions, killing indiscriminately and without a trace. The most popular scuttlebutt had it that the Stones operated with the covert sanction of the US government, since they killed so efficiently, though outside what the military liked to advertise as its game rules for warfare. Often, when someone did not return alive from a patrol, the other guys in the company would say the departed comrade had 'joined up with the Stones.' And though there was never any concrete proof of their existence, they became a legend of the Viet Nam war as well as – appropriately enough – a euphemism for death. The Stones meant death, apparently, now, in more than one language.

It made sense that hellraisers like the Stones, if they did exist, would turn mercenary and be attracted to hot spots like the Falkland Islands, El Salvador, or Chad. To run all over the globe like that they needed a lot of ordnance at home – thus a pipeline into Central America via Mexico and Houston, Sonora via Tucson, and so on.

'These weapons are popping up south of the border,' said Devon. 'Although they're legally manufactured for legitimate purposes in this country, many of them vanish, to wind up in the hands of a dead guerilla.'

'On this end it only registers as a paperwork foul-up,' Michael said. He had a good understanding of how the skim-off worked. 'Warehouses and armouries get raided, but the ripoffs never make the papers because the public would flip its collective lid if it knew four hundred M-16s and LAW rockets and SAM-7s had just walked out the door in the hands of radical crazies. Beyond that, you can have a "lost" shipment that just happens to cover enough armaments to flatten a medium-sized country, or "incomplete" records on things like surface-to-air missiles. . . .'

'Yes. Diversion into the black market is complex, but for experts, ultimately worth the risk. Most banana republics are known to pay in gold for their guns.' Devon looked at the obliterated cactus one last time. 'Shall we go back inside?'

'Somehow I knew this "range war" wasn't over a few stray cows wearing the wrong brand,' said Michael as he followed Devon up the folding steps.

'No. It's over the American 180. It's over the Nunn Nineteen, a machine gun that looks like it might replace the Uzi and the AK-47 as the workhorse of terrorists. It's over the M-161A variation on our assault rifle, the one with the 40-millimetre M-203 grenade launcher attachment. It's about the drum-fed Malko cartridge launcher with the big fat bullets.'

This last stuck in Michael's mind. He had seen the gun in a movie, thinking it was the concoction of some weapons-crazed scriptwriter or prop department. The Malko was a metal contraption that fed off a revolving drum of shells that measured, individually, nearly an inch and a half in diameter. You could 'creatively load' the thing with a combination of explosive, incendiary, fragmentation, and smoke loads and cause a one-man catastrophe in the time it took to empty maybe three clips on the American 180. This whole detour was turning into serious business.

'We're not dealing with men smuggling crates of carbines across the border,' Devon said, seeming to read what was on Michael's mind. 'This is the free release of our most sophisticated firepower into the hands of anyone with enough money.'

'Comparing that stuff to conventional weapons is like comparing KITT to a Volkswagen bug,' said Michael.

'Quite,' said Devon.

'So where do the Lagunas come in. What is a priest doing messed up in weapons smuggling – except for the convenience of having a holy man on call as your whole family gets blown to Heaven courtesy of some armaments manufacturer in Connecticut?'

'The Lagunas maintain a monopoly on just about anything of value that jumps over the border when our backs are turned. Illegal items, of course.'

'The *Sociedad Anóninia*,' said Michael.

'What?'

'The Secret Society, literally the "anonymous" society. A Mexican version of the Mob.'

'The Lagunas were well-entrenched. They controlled everything. The government and law enforcement agencies have a kind of devil's deal with them. We don't disrupt their activities; they occasionally give us under-the-table help. They helped the US. District Court nail that gangster who was living high and handsome in Arizona last year.'

'And I'm sure they had no personal interest in eliminating the competition at all, right?' said Michael with contempt.

'Either way, the Stones moved in on the Lagunas six months ago, and the bloodbath has been building ever since. We have very sketchy records on them – as well you probably know.'

'They're slippery. They have to be.'

Devon resumed his swivel seat after taking a glass of iced tea from the refrigerator. He used both lemon and lime slices, and at least five scoops of sugar. 'The Laguna family is proud and loyal, old-school blood ties, that sort of thing.' He punched a button and a silver-beaded screen on the wall lit up with a succession of rear-projected slides. The men in the slides all appeared to be in their mid-thirties, hardened and humourless. Some of the shots seemed compressed in perspective, obviously having been taken via telescopic lens. Others were as grainy and stark as mug shots.

'These men, however,' said Devon, 'are different. The "old rules," as Father Carlos put it, mean nothing to them. They've got guns to sell and to sell them, the Lagunas have to move over. The Lagunas resisted.'

Michael was examining a black-and-white close-up of a blond man with a scar bisecting his left eyebrow when the slides changed over to medium-range street shots. In the first, a man was sprawled in the middle of an urban street, chunks of his head all over the side of the Chevy Impala. Another showed the blown-in front of a barbershop with corpses in the chairs, blood darkening their bibs. The next slide featured a carload of people at a local drive-in. The safety glass was sprinkled like snow around the outside of the car, and the bodies inside were flung against the dash

22

and doors in the radical angles of death. They hadn't made it through the second feature.

'It's turning into a street war,' said Devon. 'The Stones are quite ruthless.'

Michael considered the photos some more, and turned, one hand on his chin in thought. Finally, chillingly, he said, 'So what?'

Devon's face grew puzzled. 'We need to stop the Stones, Michael. Cut the pipeline into Mexico.'

'You mean get the Stones off the backs of the Lagunas? Why? Why kill Peter to save Paul? What difference does it make if they *do* kill each other off? Is having the Lagunas run stolen American weapons into Mexico any different than having the Stones do it, besides the facts that the Lagunas owe Uncle Sam a few favours for turning the other cheek? The only difference I can see is that the Stones are better equipped.' His anger was simmering just below the boiling point at what Devon seemed to be proposing.

'The Stones are murdering innocent people,' he said, somewhat limply.

'Tell me, Devon, how many lives are the Lagunas saving by bringing in good South American dope and shipping out guns. By importing wetbacks and exporting car parts and gold?' He slapped the slide projector switch and the images blinked off the screen. 'I don't want to have anything to do with this. It stinks.'

Devon shifted in his seat, almost ready to wring his hands.

Michael fixed him eye-to-eye. 'What is it, Devon? What are you leaving out? You're being as shifty as Father Carlos, back there.'

'Michael, the truth is . . . that while we are not responsible for the actions of the Lagunas, who choose to deal with the government on occasion, we *are* responsible in a way for the actions of the Stones, who deal with no one except their warmasters and foreign banks.'

'Okay, so? Why not squash them both?'

'As I've said, the government *needs* the Lagunas, in a strange kind of way.'

Devon still wasn't revealing all. Michael tried to do a fast piece of mental arithmetic.

And the first thing that flashed into his mind was the memory of Wilton Knight, the man who had saved and changed the course of his life. Knight hated the military and had had plans appropriated by the government against his will. The whole affair with KITT's prototype a few months back, the Knight Automated Roving Robot, a car lacking the directive to preserve human life, had been an indirect result of military interference. The Army was so interested in turning KARR into a kind of urban tank that Wilton Knight hurriedly relocated his base of operations to Nevada. In the process, KARR was left behind, locked up – but not secure enough to avoid its eventual theft. Stopping KARR had been rough.

'It's a kind of blackmail, isn't it?' said Michael softly. 'If we don't help the government help the Lagunas, they've threatened to re-open the investigations into Knight Industries, right?'

'Not so simple, Michael. I said we were responsible for the havoc the Stones are wreaking, as well. By "we" I meant –'

'Knight Industries,' said Michael. 'Of course. The Stones are running ultra-sophisticated, high-tech weapons. I'll bet I only get one guess as to what labs the technology was developed in, huh?'

'I'll relate to you just one painful example,' said Devon. 'It has to do with the American 180. The laser-sighting system was designed by Knight Labs Research and Development branch to multiply the effectiveness of low-calibre, rapid-fire assault weapons like the Ingram Model 10, the gun the FBI is so fond of carrying around in briefcases. When Wilton Knight realized this he stopped development of the programme and turned his attention to deterrent "white weapons," such as KITT. Remember that KARR's original purpose was indestructibility, and from there we'd develop it to save lives, once it could save itself. By the same token, we had to develop lethal weapons in order to find ways to counteract them. But the blueprints for the gun that wound up as the American 180 were appropriated and handed over to American Research and Development and voila – the Buck Rogers gun.'

'So those weapons you mentioned before – the Malko, the Nunn Nineteen – were all Knight Industries contracts?'

'At first, yes. As you can see they got out of our hands. But we are still responsible for their conception, and so are morally responsible for all those dead people.'

Suddenly Michael saw that Devon was taking this whole affair personally, to a painful extreme, as if *he* had mowed down people in the streets. The man was obviously committed to rectifying a situation that he did not like at all, but one which he viewed as being his fault. It would do no good to lecture him about the ethics of defending one group of gunrunners against another.

It was also clear that Devon did not wish to be cornered into the even more distressing stance of having to *order* Michael to play along with a scenario neither of them liked a bit. Michael decided to spare him that.

'Just what are you looking for from me?' he said.

Devon had been prepared to defend his viewpoint. Michael's simple request threw him off guard. 'Go to the wedding reception. Get the name of the contact and use it. Convince these people you're a black market gunrunner.'

'That's not all,' Michael said tonelessly. His distaste for the choice he felt he would eventually make did not stop his mind from objecting vigorously. His hands began to clench and unclench. His sentences became clipped, almost formally polite.

'No, I'm afraid not,' said Devon. 'I want you to set up a "buy" with the Stones. We need to catch them dirty – that is, with the goods in hand – and cut the pipeline into Central America.'

'*Their* pipeline, at any rate.'

'I *know* that!' Devon snapped. 'You should know *this:* I refuse to bring up the matter of your debt to Wilton Knight, and what you might or might not do on behalf of that. We're far beyond that now, Michael, both of us!' His eyes had become flinty behind his glasses.

'At least that was a debt of honour, not a crummy setup for keeping the government crooked and the crooks legitimate, Devon!'

'You've every right to walk out,' said Devon simply. 'You've done more than we can repay already. That's what I meant when I said you've exceeded your debt to Wilton Knight.' He remained in his seat with a contrite expression on his face, masking whatever it was he really felt.

Michael's mouth snapped shut. He had been about to shout *'You're right!'* in Devon's face when Devon had pulled the dirtiest trick in his repertoire. He had actually attacked the problem from Michael's own point of view, found it repellent, and allowed him the chance to back out with no harm done.

In short, he had outfoxed Michael by agreeing with him. He had no desire to prove Devon right by storming out (even if Devon stopped the truck, his mind added. Which he hasn't yet. The sly old dog knew I'd never walk out.).

Michael did a fast little circle in the 'office' space, which was too confined for proper nervous pacing. Finally he threw up his hands. 'Well . . . no one ever told me that I'd have to exclusively do stuff I loved in connection with the FLAG programme, right? Right.'

Devon, who had known all along how their talk would go, steepled his fingers again after finishing the dregs of his iced tea.

'But it's going to take more than a name from Father Carlos to sell me as an arms dealer to anyone with a fragment of experience . . . or common sense,' said Michael. Having dispensed with the ethical qualms (though his mind was still protesting loudly, mostly because Devon had so smoothly outplayed him, and not so much because he was stepping into hazard-laden enemy territory, since simple danger was a factor he dealt with in a state of deadly calm), he proceeded immediately to practical considerations.

'My boy,' said Devon. 'I did not plan to base our entire game on the redoubtable Father Carlos.' He was looking at KITT.

'New programming?' said Michael, catching on.

'Specialized data banks on key figures in international smuggling, and details on which you can base a phony biography. Flow charts for smuggling into and out of Texas and Mexico. Priority data fetches on Stones members – what we *could* find. It all goes into KITT.' He reached for his briefcase, withdrew some tapes and papers, and directed Michael to the chair nearest him. 'Now, if I can have your undivided attention for an hour or so, we'll scan the rest of it. Then we'll drop you off for the wedding reception.'

'Let's do it fast,' Michael said. 'Before I change my mind.'

3

KITT's smooth black form shot down the freeway offramp and headed for the centre of town. Roxy Music's 'Avalon' played softly inside the cabin as Michael let KITT do the driving on AUTO PILOT, and reviewed information on the area's gunrunning history and the legend of the *Corazones de Piedras*.

The Number One video monitor featured a blowup of the blond man with the scarred eyebrow. Number Two displayed a swarthier man with a cleft chin and drooping black moustache. The ID pulls identified the first man as RICKY (NO LAST NAME KNOWN); the second, DANNY DWIGHT (REFERENCE: 'D.D.'/NO KNOWN ALIASES).

'I've seen files on jaywalkers with more information,' Michael muttered.

'Would you care to continue the data fetch, Michael?' said KITT, apparently unconcerned.

'Yeah. Give me all of it, even the trivia, even the boring stuff. I don't want anything useful to slip by.' My life might depend on it, he added to himself.

KITT complied.

While the ramp on the Knight Industries truck was being lowered, Michael had made a quick attempt at levity as Bonnie came around to watch KITT back out. Despite Devon's somewhat desperate reassurances that they had covered all the contingencies they could, Michael's mind kept flirting with the not unlikely idea that the Stones might reject his fictional persona out-of-hand, and the legacy of the new Michael Knight would end with the grinding up of his body into cat food filler. This might be the last time he'd see either Bonnie or Devon.

'Back as soon as I bust the bad guys,' he had said. 'Back in time for dinner. How do you like your steaks there, lady?'

With a prim wrinkle of the mouth Bonnie shot back, 'I've decided to become a vegetarian.'

'Oh, no you don't. Not in Texas, m'lady. In the great sovereign state of Texas, it's a sacrilege to refuse a steak!'

'Medium rare, wise guy,' she said, smiling, and the smile lit Michael up inside. *One of these days, lady* . . . he thought.

Now he was not feeling so jolly. The reality of what he was walking into had sunk in like the needle pain of a migraine headache, and he was trying to dilute his worry by drowning himself in information.

While stopped for a red light three blocks from the Del Rio Ballroom, he looked out the pilot's side window and saw an enormous chrome hubcap.

He thumbed his window down and continued looking up. The glittering hubcap was a mag wheel the breadth of a trashcan lid, and around it was a knobby offroad tyre that must have stood a good four feet high. Its treads seemed to go on for two more feet, and on top of it all, nearly ten feet above the street, it seemed, was a custom truck cab, perched on an absurdly high, jacked-up chassis, drenched in chrome and frosted with quartz-crystal C-beam lights atop a chrome roll bar. Not a semi or a tractor truck. It was a *pickup* truck, or more properly, one of those ridiculously extravagant mutant rigs Michael had heard referred to as Cowboy Cadillacs.

The broad mouths of three upward-jutting chrome exhaust pipes blatted petrochemical smog into Michael's face, and above the racketing din he heard a shouting, good-old-boy voice. He looked up, still further.

A guy wearing a straw cowboy hat with a bunch of feathers stuffed into the snakeskin hatband was yelling down at him. Michael thought the man looked as though he had crashed headfirst into a chicken, but kept this to himself. The man's muttonchop sideburns were at least as outrageous as his truck.

'Hey, boy!' the guy bellowed. 'You wanta keep that piece of Detroit junk outta my way! You're gawpin' at the fastest machine ever raised dust in Houston!'

'It's illegal to give steroids to trucks!' Michael shouted back over the guy's roaring exhaust. 'I read that in the *Houston Chronicle!*'

The big guy in the truck cab woofed laughter and swept a clutching blonde out of his way so he could get a clearer view down at Michael. 'Hey, boy!' he yelled again. He pronounced in *bo-ah*. 'You gotta lotta spunk! Wanna drag me? I'll blow that black bucket right into the next time zone!' He haw-haw-hawed at his own wit.

'Some other time, ace!' Michael returned good-naturedly, not wishing to rile the natives.

'Ace!' yelled the man above. 'That's *great!* I love that!' And then the traffic light turned green.

The guy was still yucking it up as he stomped on the pedal. The front end of the rig jumped off the ground and the rear tyres blew up a choking cloud of scorched rubber. Michael thumbed his window back up and watched some pedestrians in the crosswalk on the opposite side of the light discover the concept of speed as they leaped out of the path of the oncoming juggernaut.

Ah, Texas, he though.

The Del Rio ballroom seemed decked out for a fiesta. Banners, streamers, noise, and flowers were everywhere, as though the frivolity inside the dance hall refused to be contained and had spilled into the outside world.

The entrance to the Del Rio was a large, semicircular drive giving way to a crumbling Spanish archway – cosmetically decayed to look older than it really was – then broadened to an open court on the other side of the wall. There was a gushing fountain in the middle of the atrium, and through the archway Michael could see people gathered around it or sitting on its rim balancing plates of food. The guests flowing through the arch gave the affair the look of a cornucopia of gaiety and celebration. A small girl in a white dress secured by a broad red ribbon tossed a handful of rose petals into the air, where they floated like pink snowflakes. Circling the courtyard was a breezeway that led still further back to the interior recesses of the ballroom itself.

Parked around the perimeter of the drive were several dozen cars. Michael cruised slowly past a cherry-red twelve-cylinder Jaguar with its convertible top down, a vintage collector's Corvette Stingray circa 1960, beautifully restored right down to the custom chrome, a Rolls Royce Silver Shadow, a Mercedes, several of the new compact Cadillacs with the sewing machine motors that Japanese efficiency had shamed the American auto industry into making. But there were other cars here, too – junker Chevys, a rusting old Dodge Dart, several chopped and channelled low riders, sitting close to the pavement on big, mean tyres.

Leaning on some of the parked cars and loitering around the archway were several clots of young men laughing, joking among themselves and quietly putting down Dos Equis beer straight from the bottle. Their eyes tracked KITT as the black car slowly promenaded around the parking area, seeking an open slot.

Too many of them seemed to pat their armpits, and Michael realized they were armed to the gills. One fellow casually reached into a brown paper sack lying on its side across the hood of an old Biscayne with sun-stripes where its moulding had been ripped off – not for a brew, but probably for a machine gun.

'Lots of beady black eyes out there all of a sudden,' Michael said to no one in general.

'*Michael,*' KITT said, using the occasion as an excuse for

cutting in. *'You haven't yet completed the data bank review. Do you think it's wise to –'*

'Something I oughta know that I don't?'

'Do you like champagne?'

He was puzzled for a moment. 'Sure.'

'I'd advise you to drink it and not the water.'

'This isn't downtown Mexico City, KITT, it's Houston,' Michael said with a grin. 'In America. The USA – remember? Besides, I think a glass of bubbly would cut through the dust in my throat rather nicely.'

'Don't drink enough to cut down your reaction time.'

'Don't worry, Mom.' He saw a slot and plugged KITT into it. They were between a classic sky-blue Thunderbird and a Mercedes.

'I hear ma-rah-chas,' said KITT awkwardly.

Michael grimaced. 'I thought Bonnie did something about your Spanish. It's *mariachis.'*

'What did you get as a wedding present?'

'A sterling silver serving platter,' Michael said wearily. 'And I don't even know the name of the bride. Or the groom.' He picked up the package – glossy, opaque white paper tied with blue ribbon – and started to climb out.

'Watch out for the gentlemen with the guns,' advised KITT.

Michael patted the roof of the car. 'Don't fall in love with one of these expensive beauties and run off on me, okay?'

'I wouldn't even consider it.'

'Right.' Crazy machine. Sometimes it made Michael feel like Roy Rogers talking to Trigger. It *did* have a personality; in a nutty way, the car was his confidant, and they swapped banter like Abbott and Costello, Matt Dillon and Chester, Amos and Andy . . . sometimes the car played a dull Zeppo to Michael's smart-mouthed Groucho; other times, it was Mr Chips to his Marlon Brando delinquent. He shook his head. A very weird and unique relationship all around.

As he approached the archway, one of the younger Chicano men, wearing a grey Western-cut dress suit, stepped forward to meet him, hand extended. Michael was a little surprised, having expected instant hostility.

The smiling man grasped Michael's hand and shook it – and did not turn him loose.

'You will stand perfectly still while Guilliermo gives you a poke-and-pat,' the man said through a smile. Michael's other wrist was vised from behind. The wedding gift was gently pulled from his grip and placed on the car hood next to the paper bag on its side. There was a quick flurry of searching, professional hands.

Earlier Michael had flashed back on his police days, wishing for the comfort of a pistol holstered under his arm. Now he saw that that would have gotten him in deep trouble. He had not carried a gun and only used one rarely since becoming Michael Knight.

'Well, *de donde?*' somebody else said from behind him. '*Qué quiere?*'

'All I want is to give my best to the blushing bride and deliver my present,' said Michael. They were still hanging onto him.

'You don't got no invitation, man,' said the one in the Western-cut suit.

'Ask Father Carlos,' said Michael. 'I'll wait.' His sarcasm was lost on the group.

Over by the car, another man said something in rapidfire Spanish and the group laughed while looking at Michael, who began to feel decidedly out of his element. Now he almost wished he was having a set-to with the uneven-tempered Liberty Cox instead of this.

Michael pictured someone going to fetch Father Carlos. The priest would be telling a polite anecdote, entertaining a group. It would take several minutes to tear him away. Then he'd be stopped on his way to the arch by some other well-wisher who would use up another thirty seconds. The group that had intercepted Michael was itchy for some kind of action; he could feel the tension vibrating the air, the jittery anticipation coming out of their pores and his own. They might decide to bury him up to his neck in the sand and pour honey on his head before Father Carlos could make his polite excuses and bother to show up.

34

Three and a half minutes seemed like as many years, but Michael did not have the leisure of being able to see his watch/comlink. Father Carlos bustled through the archway. In the company of Guilliermo, talking and gesturing rapidly.

He seemed a bit ticked off.

'Enrique,' he said, standing nose-to-nose with the man in the Western-cut suit. 'I specifically told you that Mr Knight, an honoured guest of mine, would be attending, and that he would not have a formal invitation. And you subject him to this . . . disgraceful indignity!'

'Father Carlos, I –'

Father Carlos's brow hardened and he smacked the boy across the left temple. *'Callate!'* The blow was not hard, but it was undignified – Enrique might as well have been beaten by an old woman with an umbrella. The chattering guards instantly clammed up. Enrique hung his head. 'You will beg Mr Knight's pardon and hope the Lord is as merciful as he when it comes to your bad manners!'

'Pardón, Señor Knight,' said Enrique, and Michael marvelled. The guy really meant it! 'I and my men are a little – how should I say? – anxious today. We do not want anything to blacken the wedding day of Father Carlos's sister Teresa, not with the tragedy of Miguel's death so recent.'

'No hard feelings, Enrique,' said Michael.

Guilliermo handed Michael his present back with a nervous smile.

'You guys really *are* keyed up, aren't you?' said Michael.

Enrique chewed his lip and nodded. 'Yes. This is just the type of situation that the *Corazones de Piedras* would like to shoot apart. A lot of Lagunas in one place at the same time, like the fish in the barrel.'

'Yeah, well, take it easy on the *cerveza* if you're going to strut around with guns, okay?'

Guilliermo was holding up a frosty bottle of Dos Equis. *'Por Ustéd?'* he said, indicating Michael.

He glanced at Father Carlos and almost refused – but that beer looked like the sweetest thing in the world, and his achingly dry throat would thank him a million times. Enrique would have an opportunity to save a little face in front of his buddies if Michael were to drink with them and shoot the breeze for a few minutes. Father Carlos would have to wait.

The priest smiled at Michael's good form, approvingly. 'I shall wait for you by the table nearest the fountain,' he said. 'Please feel free to partake of anything we have to offer. And then I shall introduce you to my sister Teresa.'

As Father Carlos walked off, Michael noticed the reaction caused by the mention of Teresa's name. Apparently there were some heartbroken *caballeros* on the range because of her decision to get married. Michael accepted the cold bottle from Guilliermo and toasted the men.

Guilliermo and Enrique had never understood why Polish jokes were funny to gringos until fifteen minutes later. Michael soon had them all roaring. Then, having emptied his bottle, Michael collected his gift and set out to find Father Carlos.

He found him telling a much cleaner joke – politely, of course – to a small group of people near the fountain who smiled and nodded just as politely.

The priest interrupted his story when he saw Michael. 'Ah!' he said, waving him into the circle. 'Here we have a good friend of mine of recent acquaintance, and a newcomer to our town as well.' He indicated each person in the group in turn: 'Señor Paiva, Trini and Donna Ortiz, Consuelo Losada – this is Mister Michael Knight.' They greeted him and Father Carlos took his arm, pulling him closer and aiming him. 'And this, Michael, is my sister Teresa.'

Teresa was petite, dark, and attractive, and she smiled inquisitively, acknowledging Michael with a small bow of her head. 'Welcome to Houston, Mr Knight.'

Michael presented her with the wedding gift, which she placed on the table behind her, among a tottering pyramid of similar offerings.

'You have all my best wishes,' Michael said to the bride as she rejoined them.

'Then I have your happiness as well as my own,' Teresa

said, and Father Carlos smiled. Something vital and secret – acceptance, maybe – passed between brother and sister in that moment.

Michael's eyes met and held those of Father Carlos for a significant moment. The manner of the priest was substantially different than that he had displayed earlier in the day inside the church. Michael felt an almost absurd jolt of reality – the man was connected to gunrunners of old family, yet he felt a distinct liking for him. He did not feel as though he had walked into a nest of snakes – at least, not yet. Father Carlos's eyes told him that he would be given the name of the contact for the *Corazones de Piedras* very shortly . . . but all in good time, and with proper attention to form. Father Carlos had granted Michael important time with the guards; now Michael was was expected to grant an equivalent favour. He began to perceive the balance which Father Carlos applied to all his well-considered moves, and began, a little grudgingly perhaps, to admire the man for it.

Donna Ortiz, Trini's redheaded, very Irish wife, was relieved to have another Anglo join the group, and Consuelo twined her hand in Michael's and asked him what had brought him to Houston. They enjoyed polite chitchat for a while before Father Carlos appropriated Michael and excused them both from the group, promising to return forthwith.

'I spoke to the man I mentioned earlier,' said Father Carlos, scanning the ground in front of them as they strolled back in the direction of the archway.

'Do you have a name for me?' said Michael.

'You're going to help us?'

He was silent for a moment. 'So far.'

That seemed to satisfy Father Carlos. 'The contact's name is Angie.'

'I expected another man. Last name?'

'None.'

Michael clasped his hands behind him as they walked, nodding at the people who greeted them in passing. 'At least that's consistent with everything else in the file about the Stones.'

'They take great care to . . . erase their tracks,' said Father Carlos, choosing his words carefully. 'One must always expect strange and contradictory things when dealing with such as the *Corazones de Piedras*. You must take great care not to be deceived.'

'I'm a cautious person. Father Carlos. What else about Angie?'

'There is a cocktail lounge in downtown Houston called the Embers. She works there.'

'A cocktail waitress?' Michael saw he would be moving from one party to another. No more drinks, today. Stick to the cola, he thought. He was already worried that Father Carlos's informant might be a ringer planted by the Stones – and that the Angie contact was specifically designed to dispose of snoops. If the Stones were as paranoid as their reputation suggested, it was not unlikely. But Michael doubted that Father Carlos was in on it – even the Laguna end of the border smuggling.

'There is . . . something?'

Michael looked at the priest. 'Yes. This is difficult for you, isn't it?'

Silence hung between them, and Father Carlos at that moment seemed to have a dozen horrible stories, all fighting to get out and corrupt the air with their foulness. Finally, he simply closed his eyes and nodded.

Without warning, a pair of strong arms slipped around Father Carlos from behind and locked. Michael leapt back, cocking a punch, startled.

'A thousand Hail Marys or your life!' a voice commanded.

Father Carlos slithered neatly out of the bear hug, using a judo move automatically and with great precision. He laid a hard chop toward the man behind him, stopping the edge of his palm an inch from his 'attacker's' face.

Theatrically, Father Carlos said, 'If you're not right with God, I pity you, because you're about to meet him!'

Then both men burst out laughing.

Michael, still confused, watched as a large, broad-shouldered man slapped Father Carlos heartily on the bicep.

'Roberto,' said Father Carlos. 'Meet Michael Knight – a friend of ours.'

'Those we can always use more of,' Roberto said in his deep, rich voice, extending his hand.

'How do you do?' said Michael at last.

'Roberto is another brother of mine,' said Father Carlos. 'The youngest and the craziest. *Vato loco.*'

Roberto shook his head, rather like a wet Saint Bernard. 'Ah, to be Catholic is difficult enough. To have older brothers, a necessary evil.' He shrugged. '*Ay*, but to have an older brother who is a priest ... *Que Diós tenga misericordia!*' He laughed and wrapped an arm around Father Carlos, who accepted the jest.

Amidst the general merriment, only Michael heard the peep of his comlink. He discreetly asked about a washroom and Roberto directed him. To let these people see him in conversation with his wristwatch would make them unduly suspicious, and for the wrong reasons – they might suspect Michael himself of being a ringer.

The washroom of the Del Rio was tiled, hollow, smelled slightly of disinfectant, and was unoccupied.

'Yeah, KITT?'

A note of concern ran under KITT's usual calm modulations: '*Michael, I've detected the approach of a rather large truck.*'

'Delivery? Caterers?'

'*I don't think so. It's coming in the front way. I'm reading the engine heat, and it's no delivery van. I'm also reading four – possibly five – men in the truck bed.*'

'It must be showtime. Get over in front of the archway as fast as you can!'

'*On my way.*'

In the semicircular parking drive, several arriving couples were startled to see a driverless black car abruptly drop into gear and raise dust backing out. The scattered as KITT slid around and headed for the archway at top speed. Already lumbering up the other arm of the crescent was a five-ton truck with panelled sides. The billboards on the truck box read 'Rising Sun Catering/100 to 1000.'

Enrique's boys saw the car and truck coming simultaneously, and several of them broke their guns loose as Michael came running through the archway, yelling at bystanders to stay back, in some cases shoving them out of the way to the safety of the adobe and brick wall.

The truck pulled broadside to the archway and the billboard panels flipped up. Michael saw several men inside brandishing machine guns.

As they started firing at the crowd, KITT knifed to a smoking halt between the truck and the archway with his smoke dispensers blowing combat-density fog around the whole perimeter. Hot yellow sparks flared as heavy calibre slugs skipped off the car's alloy skin like tiny lightning bolts inside a miniature grey thundercloud.

Michael pushed off the decorative planter rim near the archway and tackled Guilliermo just as a line of bullet holes blew mortar out of the wall behind them at chest-level. They went end-over-end and came up behind the rusting Chevy Biscayne. Guilliermo looked behind them, then grinned at Michael. Then he hauled a Smith and Wesson 9-millimetre machine gun out of the paper bag that was still sitting on the hood of the car and began to rake the nose of the truck with bursts.

Michael watched the slugs bounce away harmlessly where they should have perforated the radiator. The truck was armour-plated.

KITT continued dumping smoke into the air until the place looked like a riot zone. *Smoke*, thought Michael – *smoke fouls lasers*. If the boys in the truck were toting American 180s, their sophisticated targeting system was in trouble. Laser beams could not spot targets through smoke, and apparently KITT had anticipated this.

Bullets ripped the snack table apart one *hors d'oeuvre* at a time. Seeing nowhere to run, Trini Ortiz dived into the fountain as holes dug their way across the concrete rim where he had been sitting with his wife Donna.

A lower chuddering noise, a .30-calibre gun perhaps, suddenly cut through the machine gun fire, and Michael watched the remnants of the tiered white wedding cake explode like a sapling hit by a buzzsaw.

Enrique's men were returning fire now, and shots from the truck came more sporadically. Most of the automobiles parked in the prime spots, nearest the archway, had been destroyed. There was an ear-compressing *crumping* noise as the gas tank of the Mercedes let go, spitting a rolling orange fireball into the air that reminded Michael of napalm. The rear end of the car came back down, smashing apart on the ground and spraying its burning parts around. The tyres of the Chevy next to it began to burn, emitting oily black smoke.

Nobody really saw the truck rev suddenly and pull out. Rather, they watched the rolling cloud of camouflaged smoke where the truck had been.

Now Michael could hear people screaming.

'Michael? Acknowledge, please, Michael?'

Michael depressed the stud on his comlink. 'Nice to know you care, buddy,' he said. 'Stay right where you are. No pursuit. We'll be lucky if the Stones don't make my car when I show up later.'

He glanced over at Guilliermo. The young man had been hit by the .30-calibre gun, and his head was distributed all over the door panels of the Biscayne.

Enrique was writhing in the dirt, several blotches of blood covering the right side of his Western suit. He was trying to stand up and kept falling down.

As the smoke dispersed, Michael looked around for Father Carlos, but it was Father Carlos who found him first.

Consuelo ran across the courtyard to Father Carlos's brother Roberto. She yanked the tablecloth out from under the ruined food like a bad amateur magician, sending a hail of snacks into the fountain. She quickly began to tear the thick white cloth into strips.

'Michael!' It was Father Carlos. 'Roberto's been hit!'

The older man caught up with him and the two ran together. 'Yeah!' Michael shouted back. 'I noticed a few people lost interest in the party all of a sudden!'

Near the fountain, Donna Ortiz was mopping blood from

41

her forearm with a wad of cocktail napkins. The napkins were decorated with silver wedding bells.

'Where's Teresa?' said Michael.

'She is safe. She and her husband Rudy were inside the ballroom when the shooting started. But others have been hurt – shrapnel, ricochets, mostly superficial, it looks like.'

'Except for Guilliermo.'

'Yes, except for the ones in front.'

Donna Ortiz was scared nearly to death by the sight of her husband rising out of the fountain behind her, calling her name. He looked like some decaying ghost, dripping wet, coated with the mulch of half-dissolved wedding cake and canapés. When she realized who was calling her, she threw her arms around him.

Consuelo was kneeling over the crumpled form of Roberto, propped up against the other side of the fountain rim. Michael could see that he had already lost a lot of blood. She checked his wounds, then stripped off her belt and cinched it tight around Roberto's upper arm.

She looked up at Michael. 'He has to get to a hospital right away. There's not much time.' There was no fear in her face – she was apparently used to dealing with crises. There was a comma-like smear of blood on her forehead.

'Let's get him up, then, Father,' Michael said.

With Consuelo holding the emergency dressings in place, Michael and Father Carlos hoisted Roberto up, gently, one on either side of him.

Now Michael did not care what they thought of the comlink: 'KITT! You still there?'

'*Yes Michael.*'

'Father Carlos – where's the nearest hospital?' They were having difficulty getting Roberto across the courtyard. Each stumbling step caused a firebolt of agony in his arm and torso.

'Mercy General,' the older man gasped. 'Just off the intersection of Principal Street and Fifth. That is where the Lagunas have been tending their wounded and dead these past few months.'

'KITT, chart the quickest route to Mercy General off

42

Principal Street and Fifth. Is that enough?'

'Laid in on the monitor. Michael, are you wounded?'

'No, but we've got somebody else who is, and we need to get him there in a hurry.' To Consuelo and Father Carlos in general, he said, 'Why the hell hasn't anybody called any ambulances?'

'The telephones in the Del Rio,' said Consuelo. 'They went dead about fifteen seconds before that truck rolled up the drive.'

'They're soldiers, alright,' Michael said. 'Cut the lines before the raid. Made sure that most of the cars that could have given chase were incapacitated. Very slick fellows, these Stones.'

Enrique was on his feet by the time they made the gate. The sight of Roberto, full of holes on one side, almost knocked him down again, with anger.

'Father Carlos!' he snapped, blinking blood from his eyes. 'The time for talking is done! When are we going to do something about the *Corazones*, eh? Guilliermo is dead!'

Father Carlos, no longer the stern, paternal figure, said, 'I'm trying, Enrique,' in a small voice. 'I am trying.'

Enrique seemed to focus on Michael then, and realized what was going on. As Consuelo and Father Carlos carefully tucked Roberto into KITT's passenger seat, he leaned very close to Michael's ear and said, 'Kill them. Wipe them from the earth. Destroy them!'

Grimly, Michael surveyed the carnage before getting into the car. 'Welcome to Houston,' he said.

4

In downtown Houston, skyscrapers thirty and forty stories high reached toward the moon. Especially popular inside the urban metroplex were those featureless corporate boxes apparently composed of nothing but mirrored glass. In Houston, spanking-new architectural nightmares seemed to spring from the ground overnight. The city was full of reflective surfaces and hard stainless steel.

KITT's glimmering black alloy hide threw back the reflections of the city at night as Michael cruised the main artery streets, looking for the Embers. It turned out to be one of the feature draws of a recently constructed – though everything downtown looked recently constructed – hotel complex called the Houston Plaza, an imposing, multiwinged building rendered in dead white with windows of black glass so dense that the individual room lights, running in neat rows upward for nineteen stories or so, were pale orange, like light bulbs about to burn out. Perched on top of the building, across from a large penthouse, was the Embers – a slowly revolving lounge/bar affording a spectacular view of the city. It looked like an enormous flying saucer of black glass with tiny pinpoints of gold light showing through as it turned lazily.

A marquee the size of a football field proclaimed the presence in the Embers of Cash Flagg and the Axemen on Fridays, Saturdays, and Sundays, Happy Hour rates, group rentals, group party rentals which included a block of private rooms in the hotel portion of the Plaza, and other incentives.

'That's the castle, KITT,' Michael said to the car. 'And I've got to storm it.'

'The Stones apparently move in a very lavish circle,' noted KITT.

'Why else do you think people fight gang wars, or mob wars? It has nothing to do with blood ties, like the movies say. The bottom line is always money. Without it, why go to all the trouble?'

'What about the Lagunas? They seem quite cohesive as a family unit. "Tight," as you might say.'

'True, buddy.' Roberto Laguna was going to live even though the fusillade of bullets broke his right arm in three places, blowing arteries and muscle tissue completely apart. The only casualty of the attack had been poor Guilliermo – the one Michael had saved from the first shots. Enrique was out of the running as a bodyguard. If KITT had not picked such as opportune time to intercede with his smokescreen blowers, there would have been just as much noise and panic, but a lot more corpses. The programmed directive to preserve human life had struck again.

At Mercy General hospital, Michael watched as Father Carlos comforted the old men, women, and children of the Laguna clan. He had been doing it a lot lately.

Once assured Roberto could benefit no further from his presence, he made to leave. Father Carlos hurried down the corridor to intercept him.

'What is your plan,' he asked, 'when you make the contact with Angie?'

'I never plan that far ahead,' Michael had said. 'I like to run on instinct. Marks can smell something phony if your lines sound too rehearsed.' He added with a smile, 'I'd just rather not talk about it.'

'Discretion is no cause for embarrassment,' replied Father Carlos, who seemed to have just such a homily in stock for every occasion.

'I'll be in touch, then,' Michael said at the door.

'Consuelo implores me to advise you to be careful. I sense that would be . . . redundant. You are a cautious man despite your brash exterior, your facade of not caring, of *machismo* toughness. Nevertheless, I too will tell you to watch out for yourself – perhaps needlessly, perhaps not – and I send my luck with you.'

'A little good karma never hurts, Father. Send Consuelo my thanks.'

'Of course.'

Michael felt the priest's eyes on his back all the way through the parking lot. He wondered what the older man might be contemplating.

If the truth be told, the Embers meeting appeared to be more of a situation in which Michael could feel at home. This was the sort of place that attracted a regular clientele of wealthy phonies, bored divorcées, ex-jet setters, and predatory hustlers; lots of flash and gilt and as little substance as possible. He could fake his way with the best *this* place had to offer.

He still hadn't got out of the car, and found he had to move his mouth to motivate himself. 'Well . . . here I go, stepping right into the jaws of death again.' He knew that if he sat much longer he'd devote too much morbid thought to the fact that the Stones and the Lagunas were essentially the same, and he might just as soon drive out of Houston, out of their lives, and out of the assignment. Devon would not be pleased.

'*Remember the comlink if anything happens,*' advised KITT, rather like a worried grandmother telling a child not to forget his galoshes.

'Monitor everything,' said Michael. 'I like to feel like my partner's right there with me, and I'll want tapes for review.'

'*Alright, Michael.*'

'Okay. Let's bring on Angie.'

'*One other thing, Michael,*' said KITT as the car door closed. '*Devon has requested hourly updates from me on your progress*'

'Squelch that idea. I don't want to get back in touch with Devon until this thing has a happy ending in sight, got me?'

'*I think so.*'

'Lie to him. Anything. I'll get in touch later.'

'*Michael,*' said KITT as he turned to leave. '*I can't lie to Mr Devon.*'

'I'm not asking you to lie. I'm asking you to tell the truth selectively, got me?'

'*I think I'll have to analyze that statement, if you don't mind, Michael.*'

'Right.' He would have slammed the car door, but it was already shut.

A triangular glass-walled elevator expressed passengers directly to the top floor, giving a stomach-lurching view of the Plaza's massive atrium. Open-air hallways rimmed the interior of the building, allowing guests to view the bizarre wrought-metal sculptures that filled up the vast airspace. They turned lazily in the backwash of the industrial air conditioners.

The centre elevator, the bullet car, was flanked by several others that gave individual floor service. All the elevators eventually terminated on the Embers level, to spare guests the embarrassment of having to take two elevators after too many martinis. There were other 'progressively designed' hotels in Houston that had, in their haste to be fashionable, overlooked such comforts.

Michael, the sole passenger in the bullet car, leaned on the wood-grain handrail and watched the floor dwindle away beneath him. On his way up he shot past another car, on the eighth floor. Its occupant, a young woman in very tight, very loud blue satin pants and an equally tight T-shirt that read 'Fort Worth is for Lovers' in glitter, watched him come and go.

A chime bonged softly and the steel-panelled doors to the

rear retracted. Michael turned and faced a nondescript wall of brown cork with a little gold arrow on it.

The arrow directed him to a corridor, which widened into a guest foyer leading back into the depths of the Embers. A harried man, obviously just out of his teens, in an ill-fitting work tuxedo looked up from his tiny reservations pulpit and said, 'Good evening, sir. Dinner tonight? A table for one?'

'I'm not sure yet,' said Michael. 'I'll fill a slot at the bar in the meantime, and if I decide to pop for dinner I'll come back and check in with you, okay?'

The young man blushed, not sure if Michael was having a joke at his expense. 'Very well.'

Michael passed him and shook his head. *Very well.* The kid must have gotten that line either from management or from the late show on television; he doubted whether his cronies from the Houston high school system talked that way to each other.

Oh, he had this place made, alright.

Every eye in the place followed him in, women appraising him as a potential mate, men sizing up possible competition, employees taking note of a newcomer (big tipper or cheapskate?), tipsy bar leaners wondering if his was a shoulder they could cry on, a nervous, heavyset guy in a blue suit who just had to be a hotel security guard. Once he found a bar stool and slid onto it, the noses all around resumed interest in their glasses and plates.

The bartender, an overweight fellow whose fat fingers made polishing the glasses look rather comical, sidled over and spoke in a typical Texas drawl: 'Waddle it be, pard?'

'Draft,' said Michael.

'You gotta preference? We got –'

'Whatever's coldest.'

'Gotcha.'

Michael affected just the right air of bored amusement as he checked out the action. Gary Numan was pulsing out of the jukebox near one end of the bar, lending a surreal air to the whole place.

The waitresses wiggled to and from the bar in painfully brief short shorts, showing a lot of leg for the customers.

Management had obviously told them *just how many* buttons on their blouses had better be undone if they wanted to make minimum wage with regular pay bumps. The waiters – they served the food, the waitresses did the alcohol – were all runners-up from a *Gentleman's Quarterly* cover model contest, it seemed, and all wore similar gear – close-fitting vests and very tight pants. Michael had not seen a menu but guessed the house specialty was an underdone steak at an overblown price.

A cocktail waitress collected a tip – wet dollar bills – from a vacant round table and checked in at the bar. She flashed Michael a smile that could have powered all the signs in Las Vegas for half an hour. He smiled and nodded in return, watching the smooth way she and her co-workers managed to step from the stationary centre of the bar to the gigantic, slow-moving carousel section of the Embers, where the dining tables were, carrying full trays and not breaking stride or looking clumsy.

The waitress was back at the bar about five minutes later. 'It's like stepping onto an escalator,' she said without looking at Michael. 'If you do it enough you get used to it. Second nature. Once they turned the floor off in here – maintenance or something – and we started falling all over the place because we're so used to the moving floor.'

'Good way for weeding out potentially dissatisfied workers,' said Michael.

'Yeah. Enjoy your beer.' And she was off.

The Embers was too hip to supply the waitresses with name tags, but Michael assumed Angie was on tonight due to Father Carlos's tip. Which one could she be? He counted at least five, slipping efficiently around in the near-dark of the restaurant/lounge.

The one to whom he had spoken – perky, hurried, short auburn hair cut in a rag, very appealing, rounded dimensions. Hazel eyes.

Another woman working the tables on the carousel. Tall, dark, coltish, Indian-looking.

One who served the smaller 'drinker's tables' inside the circle. Five-seven or five-eight, pretty little snub nose, dark eyes, big chest, and a lithe, dancer's way of weaving through the close seating and the occasional grabbing male hand.

One who wore her hair in a long horsetail braid, draped over one shoulder. Very blonde, very California, tall and tanned, with perfect teeth and jade green eyes. Her hands were slender and tapered like a pianist's, and she spoke in a low, throaty voice that pleased her customers.

Another, a bit older, with worldly eyes and a slightly bemused, tired-but-content expression. She watched the world from beneath a curly cloud of light brown hair, and had a red bandanna tied around her neck and tucked into her open shirt. She appeared to be going on her break.

In her stead came a younger woman, a girl, almost – a bit thin but attractive. Good legs, thought Michael, but she wasn't used to the heels. New employee – maybe the sister or high school wife of the guy up front?

He saw a short woman with long black hair and Oriental eyes drop the strap of a sling bag over her shoulder. She was done for the night. He had to find out who Angie was before she took off.

The burly bartender rolled up with a fresh taste and broke a twenty of Michael's, fanning the bills across the bartop like a poker hand.

'You can keep the change,' said Michael.

'Oh yeah?' said the barkeep, sweeping the bills back. 'Mighty nice of you. I don't suppose I have to do anything for this?'

'Like what?'

'Like, maybe, answer a trivial question?'

'Does this happen to you a lot?' said Michael with a grin. He was beginning to like this guy.

'All the time. Are you kidding, a place with waitresses that look like the ones we got?' He polished a highball glass slowly and methodically. *'What's her name?* is the one I get the most, and that's nice, because I get a lot of money I don't have to give up to Reagan's tip tax law, and the girls know how to handle themselves. They never go out with customers. Well, rarely – most of these guys are all flash and

51

no cash, or all cash and no brains. You still want to ask me a question?'

Michael laughed. The auburn-haired waitress collected a drink tray from the bar and shared his smile without knowing why.

'Her name is Filene,' said the bartender. 'Happy now?'

'She's sweet, but she's not what I'm looking for.'

'What's wrong with her?'

'Nothing. I'm sure she's a great dancer and donates regularly to the humane society.' Michael downed the rest of his beer.

'Then who do you want to know about?' The barkeep ditched the highball glasses, produced a martini glass as if by magic, and resumed polishing.

'Of these people, I don't know. All I know is a name. Angie.'

'That figures,' said the bartender.

'Well?' Michael's eyes followed the waitress who was just leaving. 'That's not her walking out, is it?'

'No way. Why do you want to talk to Angie – does she know you?'

'Not yet, but yeah, I need to talk to her.'

'You'll be wasting your breath, but it's the tall blonde with the braided hair. Hang on a sec.'

The barkeep moved away as Michael immediately turned and tracked the waitress serving the drinker's tables. When she switched trays at the opposite end of the bar, the bartender engaged her in a brief conversation. In the backbar mirror Michael saw her glance over at him once, twice. Another question to the bartender. And then she came over to where he sat.

From the other end of the lounge, the shorter waitress, the one to whom Michael had spoken, suddenly got very interested in what was going on, and intercepted the bartender, asking him a few heated questions which Michael could not overhear. All at once, the blonde blocked his view of that part of the bar.

At a distance she was attractive. Up close she was even better; she even *smelled* beautiful. Oh boy, thought Michael

– you're gonna have to be *real* careful.

'Looking for me, cowboy?' she said.

'I'm looking for Angie,' Michael said. 'And I'm anything but a cowboy.'

'Oh, I don't know. I bet we could convert you pretty quick. I thought you had that out-of-town look.'

'You *are* Angie, right?'

'I can be whoever you want me to be. I'm partial to "Angie." What do I call you?'

'Michael.'

'Well, Michael,' she said, folding her hands on the bartop and fixing him with her hypnotic green eyes, 'since I have no idea who you are, maybe you'd better start by telling me why you want to talk to me. I presume you weren't just struck by the thunderbolt of my incredible beauty when you walked through the door?'

Filene huffed past them and Michael tried not to notice. The one with the bandanna was watching them now, too – they probably made sport of how their sisters dispatched the amorous would-be daters in such a place.

'Who gave you my name?' she said.

'A friend of a friend,' returned Michael.

She appeared to think about this for a minute, then looked him up and down once, clinically. 'And what did my friend say I could do for you, Michael? Obviously you don't need to try to pick up cocktail waitresses to get girls.'

'Well, that depends on the cocktail waitress, doesn't it?' She smiled a bitter little smile at that and he pressed on. 'It has to do with my hobby.'

'Which is?'

'Gun collecting?'

'Not girl collecting?' She seemed a bit let down.

'I'm looking for some weapons that are collectible due to their . . . uh, unique qualities.'

Angie's eyes narrowed with suspicion. 'I don't have *any* idea of what you're talking about.'

'Wait a minute; listen to me. There's a certain *type* of gun I'm interested in. I was given your name. I can certainly make anything you can do worth your while.' He made

53

rings on the bartop with his empty pilsner glass.

'My while is worth more than money, boy – this is Texas. And I don't know you.'

'Call me a businessman.'

She rolled her eyes. 'Every piker in this state thinks he or she's a *businessman*.' She said it contemptuously.

'My business is weapons. I'm sort of to munitions what the Yellow Front is to the discount stereo business.'

'You sure are subtle,' she joked. 'So who is it that gave you my name?'

'He's out of the racket now – too hot. You don't know him, I think.' He grabbed the first name his head could invent. 'A guy by the handle of Kitt Worth. He used to do business with the Lagunas. He told me the Lagunas are old news, on the way out, and that if I was coming down here I should get in touch with you, because you knew the people who were on the way in.'

'I never heard of that guy.'

'Hey, Angie, I'm just asking you to make a phone call; get me an introduction. Or get me somebody else I can talk to. Somebody who'd like to make some real cash instead of loitering around a cocktail joint in a goose-me suit and spike heels.' That stung her a bit, and that was what he wanted. It was best not to appear too willing. 'If I'm not for real, your people will know. And if you didn't know who I'm talking about you wouldn't be so jumpy. You let them do their job. You do yours. My commission rate on the average buy is five percent. For your help I'll bump it to ten on anything I purchase.' He waited a beat, to allow her time to do some addition in her head, then put in, 'For the kind of bulk I buy in, that could mean anywhere from fifteen to twenty grand for a little bit of your time. You rich enough you can't afford to consider that?'

She drummed her sculpted fingernails on the counter. 'You stay here. Have another beer on the house. I'm going to go make a phone call.'

'Thanks.'

'Don't thank me, yet. If I come back in here in ten minutes, I want you to leave a *huge* tip on the bar and blow town, and never show your face in here again.'

'And if you're not back by —' he consulted his comlink. 'Nine forty-five?'

'Then meet me in the lobby of the Plaza.' She turned and left, speaking briefly to the bartender.

The barkeep brought over a complimentary beer. 'Wow. Don't know how you did it, son, but you just broke a house record. Angie never goes out with anybody.'

'Just charm, I guess.' It was 9:40.

Nine forty-five came, and Michael went. Filene glared forlornly at him as he left, and Michael felt a bit sorry for that.

5

'Mind if I turn on the radio?' said Angie, scanning KITT's Super Dash, unsure of where the radio actually was.

'Feel free,' said Michael.

She had been sitting on the arm of a sofa, inside a cluster of couches that formed one of many social groupings scattered around the vast lobby, letting her legs distract passers-by and privately enjoying it. She had not changed out of her uniform, and in the brighter light of the Plaza's main hall Michael saw that it was even more revealing. The ruffled, open-throated blouse was very sheer, the hot pants very tight, and her legs would have been sensational even without the pantyhose or the heels. She was idly smoking a cigarette, and did not stand up as he crossed the lobby to meet her.

'You have a car?' she said, blowing a smoke ring. She had unwrapped herself from her brief, basic black waitress apron, and it was draped over the sofa arm beside her, full of pens and tip money.

'I'll drive you out and back, of course,' Michael offered.

'My car is in the employee lot. You can drive me out but

you probably won't have to drive me back. I can cadge a ride.' She butted her cigarette in a silver pedestal ashtray full of white sand and led him outside.

They had exchanged maybe ten words since, and now she was fiddling with the radio. Talking was making her uncomfortable. Now she was behaving much more like some salaried minor functionary with an unpleasant job to do. Michael smelled the makings of a trap of some kind.

Jolly, weird Mexican party music danced out of KITT's cabin speakers, filling the car with its *boompa-boompa* calliope beat. Michael suppressed a grin. Angie punched the selector button and only got more of the same – on all channels, apparently.

'Weird looking radio,' she said, digging for another cigarette.

Michael nodded. Let her lead for a while, he thought.

'Weird looking dashboard, too.'

One is either born to Mexican dance music, or finds that after five minutes of listening that it will never do anything for you. Angie switched off the radio, annoyed that she could not use it to avoid confronting the stranger in the seat next to her. Michael sensed she was ready to pop, and perhaps talk a little closer to the truth.

She missed with her match and had to light up a second time. She glanced at Michael. And finally she spoke.

'Off the record, okay?'

He nodded.

'The people you want to do business with are bad. I mean seriously bad. Like killing bad.'

'I sort of got that impression,' Michael said, holding in his mind an image of the wipeout at the Del Rio Ballroom just a few hours earlier.

'I just hope you are who you say you are . . . and not some kind of . . . I don't know, Fed or something.' She pondered this, then added, 'You don't look like a Fed.'

'You always this suspicious?'

'You bet your weird dashboard, cowboy. When it comes to this kind of business, you're suspicious or you're not breathing.'

More tough talk. Michael imagined it came from hanging out with animals like Ricky No-Last-Name and Danny Dwight, AKA D.D.

'I hate it,' she said.

This was it, thought Michael. He was about to see either a piece of the real Angie . . . or the opening act of a cunningly constructed deception. She wasn't warning him just to try to scare him anymore.

'What?'

'This kind of . . . business. Makes you feel kind of unclean.'

'Then my next question should be fairly obvious,' he said. 'Why are you in it?'

'I'm not "in it." I just happen to know people who are, that's all.'

Without really meaning to, Michael said, 'Yeah, that's like the line everybody gets in high school, remember? Nobody has VD, but everybody knows somebody who does.' This tack would probably just make her defensive, and that was not a great idea . . . but Michael also had his own conscience to contend with.

She was staring absently out the window now, at the desert night and the barren countryside.

Scrub and sand flew past. Sometimes, if you were driving out here late enough, your headlights would catch and hold the silver eyes of some desert creature, just long enough to make you think you'd seen an Indian ghost. It was compelling and spooky, the way the stretches of sand and ragged high-temperature flora became claustrophobic and haunted at night. At high noon, temperatures leapt over the hundred mark; at midnight it got so cold that you needed three blankets and a fire.

The desert provided another service. If they were really going to see a couple of the Stones tonight, then Michael realized that their meeting place was inside a sterile cordon of desert . . . and a lot of nothing else. The distance of wasteland between the Embers and the meeting place – wherever it might be – was rather like a moat, a buffer zone of insulation. If there was trouble, an escaping car could be easily hunted and run to ground; and if the escapee had no car, the task became even easier. Rather like a hunt on a fenced preserve. If the hunters did not bag their prey, the environment would do it for them, just as soon as the glaring orange globe of the sun peered over the horizon.

They passed a billboard with the cryptic phrase '100 Per Cent Indian/10 Miles Ahead.'

'Grab a left,' said Angie, and Michael saw a posted dirt road just past the sign.

Further off to the left floated a small oasis of light. Other than KITT's high-beams, it was the only light around. The absence of ambient city light out here made billions of stars brightly visible.

As they approached, Michael made out a large ranch house surrounded by grounds lights and palm trees – very fancy. Very expensive.

They rolled carefully along the mostly dirt access road. It was more used to trucks and four-wheel drive vehicles than urban machines. They passed a silver barn-sized mailbox.

'So what kind of car is this, anyway?' she said, attempting to lighten up and shift subjects. She kept crossing and uncrossing her long legs needlessly. She was nervous.

'Custom-made,' said Michael. 'I dig gadgets. Where do we turn in?'

'Right up here, somewhere . . . uh, there.' She pointed with her cigarette.

'What do they grow out here?' Michael said. The house was obviously smack in the middle of a large tract of farmland.

'Nothing.'

'Is this one of those subsidy farms that gets paid to grow nothing?'

'All I know is there hasn't been a crop for several years.'

'Tired,' said Michael. 'I think we've arrived.'

It was like a duplicate of the scene at the Del Rio ballroom. A ragged U-shape of parked cars, with enough brand names in the bunch to impress tenderfeet. There was a selection of Jeeps, Broncos, Rangers, Eagles, and several subspecies of Cowboy Cadillac, as well. As far away from the house as the parking lot was, Michael could still hear the strains of Roy Clark's corny 'Thank God and Greyhound You're Gone' flooding forth from an undoubtedly expensive PA system.

'Sorry I didn't bring my Stetson.'

'It wouldn't help. Come on, let's get this over with.'

Funny, thought Michael. She should be a lot happier, looking forward (as she must have been) to collecting a substantial commission. She talked more like a sale was not the issue . . . and maybe a quick body-disposal was. Michael's guard was primed and up.

Halfway across the lot, Michael slapped his head.

'Damn it!' He half-turned back toward KITT. 'I forgot to lock up.'

She looked at him from the corners of her eyes. 'I thought your car did everything.'

'Not until they invent a gadget that locks the doors without locking in your keys. And not until I install it. See how complicated it gets?' Without begging her leave he trotted back to the car.

KITT, having overheard everything, unlocked the driver's side door so Michael's ruse was alibied.

'*I presume you have something to tell me away from the presence of the young lady?*'

'You got it. I want the licence plate number of every car at this bash; patch them all through to Devon's computer and see if any of the names cross-match with what we've got on the Stones.'

'*About that young lady,*' KITT put in. '*I do not have a "weird looking dash." I'm proud of my da –*'

'Just get the licence numbers and don't take it personally, okay?'

'*Don't forget about Emile Pavlon.*'

'Right. Thanks for the tip.'

'*De nada – how's that?*'

'Not bad. Hang around here long enough and you'll be better at it than I am.'

Michael made a show of closing the door and jiggling the handle. Then he returned to where Angie waited, tapping her foot.

Even in her waitress uniform, dramatically backlit by the house at the end of the walk, Angie looked terrific. She ushered Michael up the walk and into the party taking place inside. The goon in the extra-large suit (and eleven-gallon hat) at the door recognized her and waved them in, and when they entered together they turned heads.

Inside, Michael found a louder and slightly younger version of what he had encountered at the Embers – an overdose of noisy Texas chic. Too-hip urban cowboys and girls with serious suntans and show-off jewellery; people who defined beauty solely in terms of youth and physical firmness, if not fitness. Drones in designer jeans and Tony Lama boots made moves on vapid, busty women who squeaked and giggled at lines that had been used hundreds of times at hundreds of other parties.

The stereo had been set up by a show-off who had ensured that each room would be equally drowned in obnoxious country-and-western music; a different simultaneous tune for each room. There was a clawfoot tub in the centre of the living room filled with iced bottles of champagne and cans of cheap American beer. A moose head hung over the fireplace with a woman's red silk bra strung between the antlers. Bright-eyed young lovelies discreetly snorted cocaine through rolled hundred-dollar bills or off the wrists of their dates-of-the-moment.

Angie touched Michael's arm. 'I'll announce our arrival. It'll take a few minutes to set things up. Have a beer, okay?'

Michael kept his eyes on her as she waved and dodged through the multitude and vanished down a hallway.

Outside, beyond sliding glass doors on the patio by the swimming pool, some partygoers were setting up an impromptu wet T-shirt contest. Small circles of people were trying to out-shout each other over the blaring music. A young woman in a tight white buckskin skirt was curled up on a bearskin rug before the cold fireplace, sound asleep or passed out. People stepped easily over her as though she were just another piece of furniture. Beyond the bathtub, for the pickier of the throng of moochers, was a wet bar staffed by three women in costumes similar to Angie's, all displaying thighs, smiles, and cleavage to best advantage.

A tall dude in a cowboy hat danced slowly, wrapped up in his date, oblivious to the commotion all around them.

Somebody made an embarrassed, strangling noise and made a break for the hallway – and presumably, the bathroom.

Wings of the ranch house went off in three directions from the central room. Michael moved toward one to get out of the traffic flow and casually opened up the first door he found at hand. The room was dark inside, but when the door opened he saw a bedsheet flash up over a tangle of mostly naked people, accompanied by several screams that broke apart into wild laughter.

Michael closed the door and did not open any others.

'Lose your date?'

The hand grasping Michael's shoulder had long, buff-coloured nails and a large diamond ring. It was not a wedding ring.

The woman's face was framed by a leonine mass of wavy black hair that fell generously around her shoulders, and featured, as contrast, eyes of a penetrating ice-blue colour. She spoke with a faint British lilt. And her hand stayed where it was.

'Uh – no, not exactly,' Michael said, disoriented.

'What then, exactly,' she said with a leading little smile. Though the cacophony in the room was tremendous, she seemd to be speaking just above a whisper, but Michael caught every word. Her lips were frosted, her smile almost too much to take in at once.

'She'll be back. She just went to . . . er, check on something.'

The woman nodded, as though she was privy to some joke Michael could not understand. 'Honey,' she said. 'People at these things are always running off to check on something, or freshen up, or see a man about a steer. She's probably bopping in one of the bedrooms or checking out the drug of her choice. Don't worry about her; she'll show up. In the meantime, my name's Roxy and I'm pleased to meetcha.'

Her arm slipped around Michael's waist and the temperature in the room seemed to rise ten degrees.

Michael looked around. Still no Angie. Was it a set-up, or worse, a ditch? He felt a sudden urge to rush outside and check the parking lot.

He raised his hand to run it through his hair, bringing the comlink close to his face. With his face pointed away from Roxy – as though he was casually surveying the room – he said, 'KITT, has Angie left the house?'

'*No, Michael.*'

'Excuse me, love – what did you say?'

'Nothing,' Michael said. 'Just a mumble.'

'*Michael?*' said KITT, confused. '*Who's that? Come in, Michael.*'

'There's a voice coming out of your wristwatch,' said Roxy.

'No, there isn't,' said Michael.

'*Michael?*' It was KITT again, being a pain.

'Cool it, KITT.'

KITT accepted that as an acknowledgement, but Roxy said, 'I'm not kid, lover, and I never cool it. You'll see.' She looked again at the comlink. 'Is that one of those darling little Japanese watches that talks?'

'Something like that,' said Michael. Making sure KITT overheard, he added: 'One of the cheap ones. It's really embarrassing sometimes; always butting in, announcing the time and playing "Amazing Grace" in the middle of a funeral, that sort of thing.' Let KITT do a slow burn on *that* one, he thought.

'Why ever did you buy such a thing?' said Roxy with an endearing little frown.

'I didn't. It was a present. I'd already got twenty neckties and I own one suit.' Still no Angie. What was happening?

'I notice your girlfriend hasn't returned yet,' Roxy said, divining his thoughts. 'Or is she your wife? Nice, but no taste in clothes.' Roxy was spray-painted into a revealing evening gown slit high and low.

'She's not my wife,' said Michael.

'Thank God for the favours of fate,' she replied. 'Let's go out of this close crunch and all these sweating bodies. Everybody's trying to hustle everybody else in here. Let's go out by the pool and fight to make this conversation more interesting, shall we?'

Business and pleasure fought a mock war inside Michael's skull. He knew all along which had to win.

Roxy was pulling his arm, leading him, when his other arm was grabbed and pulled the opposite way.

'*Excuse* us,' said Angie, her eyes smouldering.

'Bad timing, love,' Roxy said, relinquishing Michael's hand. 'I'll wait by the pool. But not too long, you understand.'

'I'm sure he's just palpitating. Come on, Michael.'

'Michael. Nice name,' Roxy said as Angie led Michael toward the hallway.

'Keeping yourself entertained?' Angie said pointedly.

'After I conclude my business, I'm free for the evening,' Michael said simply, affecting the air he imagined a highpower gunrunning type might use to impress everyone – disdain and reckless availability. 'And I haven't noticed any other offers yet.'

'Spare me,' she said.

They pushed past people and made for the master bedroom at the end of the wide hallway. The music faded to a basso thumping behind them.

'In here,' she said, opening the door.

'Oh, after you.'

'Sure.' She stepped inside, and Michael followed.

A callused hand clamped on Michael's throat and yanked him forward. He heard the door slam. The vicelike hand lifted Michael off the floor and slammed him into the foyer wall opposite the door. Before he could react, something hard and cold that was definitely a wide-bore gun barrel was shoved against his adam's apple.

He looked down into the maniac face of Ricky No-Last-Name, eyebrow scar and all. Ricky spoke.

'You blink without my say-so, cowboy, and you'll live just long enough to watch your brains get airborne.'

6

Michael recognized the Stones thug named Ricky from the mug shots, and faster than he could get his bearings, realized that he was being patted down by D.D. For the second time that day he was thankful that he had not packed a gun.

He was swiftly searched. D.D. was good at it.

'You know,' he said as far as his constricted throat would allow. 'The last dude who tried something like this spent a whole month trying to get his kneecaps out of his nose.'

'Yeah, yeah, you're a real big man,' muttered D.D. 'He's clean, Ricky.' The bigger man – D.D. – backed off; the grip on Michael's throat relaxed a notch as Ricky leaned in for his first question.

'We have something in common,' he said to Michael in a low, serpentlike hiss. 'The last guy who tried to make us quiver in our boots by talking tough got kind of, you know, *separated* into little bits and pieces and fed to the local buzzards. I personally dropped his head into the Gulf of Mexico in a shopping bag. You ready for another trip to the Gulf, D.D?'

The man with the droopy moustache laughed roughly.

Michael tried for an expression of annoyed distraction as he pushed Ricky's hand away. 'Listen: I'm a professional. I assumed you guys were too. I didn't drive all the way out here in the dark to get patted down and jerked around.' As he spoke, he hoped KITT was reading everything via comlink and recording voiceprints for the two ringleaders of the Stones.

'In that case,' said Ricky, moving back, 'you're either very good or very foolish. It'll take us about five minutes to find out which.' His hand drifted directly from Michael's throat to Angie's waist. She allowed it to slither around her tolerantly, but not with pleasure. He crushed her against him.

'Ricky,' she said, the bright panic in her eyes visible only to Michael. 'I'd rather wait outside, huh?'

'We can all have a little man-to-man talk,' said D.D. He was clearly interested in finding out what he wanted to know by violence.

'She brought him; she stays,' said Ricky.

D.D. reholstered his piece. Michael saw that it was a big, silver autoloading Magnum, a cannon that weighed nearly four pounds when loaded with eight 240-grain Magnum cartridges. That pistol wouldn't have blown his head off – it would have vaporized it along with the wall behind it.

Ricky wandered across to a dresser and knocked out three fingers of bourbon into a water glass, then slugged down half in one gulp. 'Angie, go get the gentleman a cold beer or something. He's sweating like a pig.' His eyes moved away from Angie, his hands released her, and it was suddenly as if she did not exist. Michael now saw that Ricky was packed as well – in his case, a vintage World War II German Schmeisser submachine pistol was cinched tight beneath his left armpit. These guys had the artillery, all right.

Ricky sniffed, muscles expanding beneath his weight-lifter's jersey. 'Angie tells us you're in the market for some, ah – collector's items.'

Michael decided the coolest route was to let everything pass. 'Yeah.'

'Who said we had what you're looking for?'

D.D. moved away and sat on the bed, rather like an attack dog waiting for a command.

'Pavlon. Emile Pavlon.'

Ricky and D.D. looked at each other.

Ricky destroyed the rest of his bourbon. 'You know Emile, huh? A buyer or an accomplice?'

'We worked together once or twice,' said Michael.

'How's he doin'?' prompted D.D.

'Not so great. He's still in Torreon.'

To D.D., Ricky said, 'That's the federal prison in Guatemala. What a mess down there.' To Michael, he said, 'That where you met Emile?'

'Obviously not, because I'm sitting here, and if I'd got out of a hellhole like Torreon alive, I would've brought Emile. We were friends.'

'Where'd you meet him, then?'

Michael was grateful for the completeness of KITT's data fetch on Emile Pavlon. It had allowed him to construct a plausible charade based on one man that the Stones would not bother double-checking – a man vulnerable to slipups in foreign countries, like themselves, and thus a man who was occasionally without a forwarding address.

'Sabana Grande. A little ditch-hole of a town on the southern border of Puerto Rico. A real dump. That was in mid-'79. Emile was running Uzi submachine guns and Russian assault rifles into Belize by the double truckload. He had more business than he could handle, so I handled some of it. He mentioned working with the Stones in 'Nam, Danny Dwight in particular.'

D.D. nodded. 'The Hui Tan province. What a screwup. The Cong were blowing us away with bullets made in backyard puddling furnaces.'

'What else did he say about the Stones?' pressed Ricky.

Michael allowed himself a slight smile. 'That your prices were too damned high.'

Ricky sighed heavily, like a man with boring business to get out of the way. 'I don't know,' he said. 'You got weapons contacts like Emile, why do you need to see us, here in the heart of Texas?'

Michael had a prepared answer for that one, too. 'You know Emile's been in Torreon close to a year. Gunrunning isn't like competition between supermarkets to see who has the best vegetable section. I can't use Emile's direct Central American contacts because they don't know who I am.'

'But you came here,' said D.D. 'And you don't know who we are. And we don't know who *you* are.'

'I came to you guys because of the second half of my problem. I don't have any stock.'

'Why not?'

'I got burned in El Salvador, really bad. I had to do some swamp hacking just to get out of the country in one piece.'

'What were you running?' said Ricky. Michael recognized the interrogation tactic used by the two men – they were ping-ponging him between them with rapid-fire questions, hoping to see a slip or weak patch in his story.

'Mostly Smith and Wesson machine guns, LAW rockets. A crate or two of American 180s when we could liberate them.'

'Good weapon,' said D.D.

'It got me across the border,' said Michael, letting their imaginations work a bit.

'Emile still got that tattoo on his arm?' said Ricky abruptly.

Michael was ready. 'Which arm? He's got the flaming skull with the dagger on his left arm – the muscle, the bicep – and the crocodile around his right forearm like a bracelet.'

'What does it say under the crocodile?' said D.D.

'*Cocodrilos de Sudoeste.*'

'What have you got in mind?' Ricky followed, quickly.

'Nunn Nineteens,' said Michael. 'American 180s if you've got 'em. Malko cartridge launchers. Any kind of surface-to-air stuff; they need a lot of that.'

'Who needs it?'

'The Lebanese. You guys have got South America; I don't want to cut into your market.'

'Smart boy,' said D.D. 'Ricky's already told you about the last guy who tried acing us out – the shopping

70

bag man.' He chuckled.

'The Nunn is a good assault rifle; I'm surprised these foreigners can figure out how to reload them.' Ricky came closer, enumerating items on his fingers. 'The Nunns and the American 180s we can supply right away. No dice on the Malkos; we're keeping a thread around them for now because they're in such demand. The missiles will take time but we can do that, on a smaller scale.'

'How many have you got?' said Michael.

'Within two days I can get you . . . let's see . . . twenty boxes of the Nunns, eight copies per box. Two crates of the 180s; five to a crate.'

'How much for just the Nunns?'

'Fifteen hundred a copy. Two hundred and forty grand for all twenty cases – that's cash.'

'No discount?' said Michael, eyebrows up.

'You want discounts, go buy a K-Mart machine gun,' said Ricky.

D.D. motioned Ricky over, and whispered something in his ear, briefly.

Ricky straightened. 'Tell you what. You get the cash by tomorrow, we'll have the guns a day early. I bet you don't want to hang around town, right?'

'Houston's charm leaves a lot to be desired,' Michael said, thinking back on the events of the past twenty-four hours.

Angie returned with several dripping beer cans. It was obvious she had tried to avoid coming back, and that she was not certain she wouldn't find Michael's dead body when she opened the door.

'We'll be ready by the time you get the cash,' said Ricky. 'When you're ready, contact Angie here.' As soon as Angie set the cans down, Ricky grabbed her again, his hands wandering over her body. 'For now, pop a can, huh? Wouldn't want to let a business partner go thirsty.' He said such things with one side of his mouth drawn up in a rictus-like sneer. A man like Ricky No-Last-Name had *no* friends and few partners.

Michael's throat cried out for the sweet wetness of the

brew, and despite all the alcohol he'd put down in one day – all in the course of duty – he was both perfectly sober and thirsty as a horse. An adrenal rush had blown the alcohol in his bloodstream instantly out through his pores in the form of nervous sweat. He couldn't recall being this agitated over a slip while under cover since the sting operation that had killed his partner Muntzy, way back when. But the Stones had bought his little fiction . . . for the present.

'Hey,' said D.D., motioning for Michael to toss him a can. He caught it easily, so as not to fizz up the beer, then clicked cans with Michael in a mocking little toast. Ricky continued to pursue Angie, absently. She finally wormed out of his grasp and put a little distance between them.

'What about the American 180s?' said Michael after a long sip.

'We do the Nunns first, then we talk high-tech stuff, if that's okay with you, ace,' said Ricky firmly.

'As long as you've got them.'

'We'll bring a couple tomorrow, so you can check out the stock. They're first rate.' Ricky looked to D.D. for confirmation; D.D. nodded affirmatively.

'Sounds solid,' said Michael, getting up.

'What about you, sweetness?' Ricky said to Angie, making another grab.

'I'm busy tonight, Ricky.'

'Aw, give me a break!' he said with a snort. 'Hang around the party awhile; suck up the freebies . . . unless you got some kinda date with the big, bad gunrunner here.' He indicated Michael.

'I just gave the lady a ride,' Michael said, thankful for the chance to get Angie in a spot of hot water to pay her back for the treatment he'd received earlier.

'I have to wash my hair or something. I gotta go, Ricky, sorry. Some other time.' She turned to go and paused at the door. 'Besides,' she added. 'The big bad gunrunner's not interested in me. Roxy's already tried to drag him off once tonight.'

Boom – the door closed and Angie was gone.

D.D. was laughing. 'That Roxy's insatiable. Careful

around her, man.'

Michael sank his hands into his coat pocket. 'Sounds like the party's still going full blast.'

Ricky moved across the room and stared out the windows, seemingly disinterested in chitchat.

D.D. nodded. 'Yeah. It'll go on that way until the sun comes up. Everybody gets insensate. It's tempting for a poor white boy like me, you know? I still got the urge to go steal all their tapedecks and stuff while they're laying around passed out.'

'Small time stuff for a member of the Stones, isn't it?' said Michael.

'I dunno. You pick up your change where you can get it. Sometimes you need the change, not the big stacks of cash. Dollar bills don't get you on the city bus in Houston; you've gotta have exact change – you get my meaning?'

'I think so.' Michael didn't care.

'You hangin' around for the party?'

'No. Have to get back to the city if I'm gonna collect the cash you guys want. Busy day tomorrow.'

D.D. grinned; it was not particularly appealing. 'For both of us, man.'

As Michael moved towards the door Ricky remained where he was, apparently oblivious to everything except the desert night outside.

'Is he mad or something?' said Michael, cocking a thumb toward the man.

D.D. looked for a moment. 'Naw. Ricky's convinced he's part Indian, man. Really into Carlos Casteneda. He goes into these trances sometimes; see visions, really weird stuff like that. He claims that's why we never have to worry about getting caught. He's got some kinda third Injun eye lookin' out for us in the ozone.'

Michael wasn't sure whether it was a put-on or not. He shrugged; opened the door. They physical pressure of the country music beat shoved its way into the room.

'Later, then.'

'Catch you *mañana*, man.' D.D. locked the door once it was closed. He was once again alone in the room with

Ricky. 'Well?' he said.

Ricky spoke in the direction of the window. 'Keep an eye on Angie. I'm starting not to trust her.' His tone was authoritative now, not at all the boisterous tough-guy. After a beat he added: 'Take some petty cash for enquiries. Call Jacob in Mazatlán. I want to grease Emile Pavlon out if it's at all possible.'

'Buy him out of jail in Torreon?'

'If that's not possible I want a courier. We have to check with Emile to find out if this guy's on the line or not. We have no time. Do it now.'

'Gotcha,' said D.D.

Ricky still faced the black sheet of glass and the cold night beyond. 'Do it now,' he repeated.

Michael ducked and weaved through the partygoers, keeping an eye out for Angie. She was not to be found in the main living room or any of the crowded dens.

Wearied, he downed a plastic glass of ice water from the bar, using it to wash down a couple of aspirin. He was shifting into tension fatigue.

Satisfied that Angie had in all likelihood blown the premises, he started to work back toward the front door. Noisy partygoers jostled and laughed. He zeroed in on the large bouncer in the enormous cowboy hat and moved toward him like a shipwreck victim swimming for a buoy.

He wondered about Angie's relationship to Ricky No-Last-Name. Perhaps there was a chink there he could exploit – she obviously disliked him but felt compelled to play up to him. If Michael proved sympathetic, he might gain the type of trivia that regularly saved his own life. Ample chance to work on strategy, he thought – they had committed her to seeing him the next day.

He found his way to the front door, and in giving the clamorous party one farewell glance he saw the spectacularly endowed Roxy leading another fish down one of the hallways. She glanced back his way but did not see him.

The air outside was refreshing. A quick overview told him that Angie was not loitering around the parking lot. She

74

had escaped for the night.

He walked toward KITT, thinking of nothing but the safe anonymity of his hotel room, and the bliss of deep, dreamless sleep.

7

A dusty 1972 Mustang fastback – a beautifully restored relic of the days just before the Arabs decided to usher in the age of the economy car – roared down the highway, raising a fine tail of grit, its headlights the only illumination for miles. Hunched over the wheel, dry tears smearing her mascara, was a woman with long blonde hair and striking jade-green eyes, still clad in her cocktail waitress outfit.

Angie, she thought to herself, *you sure have a way of getting yourself into the soup.*

More lately than ever, she despised her links to the *Corazones de Piedras,* particularly the fact that those links brought her in close contact with slimeballs like Ricky and Danny Dwight. Ricky couldn't keep his mitts off her; that was another recent development. Although he was handsome in an over-muscled, beachboy way, the muscles seemed to extend up onto his face and solidify in a spiritually ugly way. Maybe that was it – Ricky had one of the ugliest *minds* Angie had ever encountered. Around the Stones hung a perpetual circle of weirdos – like those at the party – and dangerous psychopaths (again in the Ricky mode; more Vietnam vets with chips on their shoulders and monkeys on their backs), people whose motives were so strange and scary that they shook Angie's commonsense faith in human nature – what she thought of as normal human nature, anyway.

This guy Michael, for example. A total cipher. How else to explain a gunrunner who was, in every way, thanks to the mere *fact* of the gunrunning, as much of a creep as Ricky . . . yet who seemed to be a nice, agreeable guy. He had even known some of Ricky and Danny's slimy partners from South America – had even contributed to that horrible business in El Salvador!

That was not what really scared her, she admitted. What shook her was the idea that she could have read someone so wrong. For a self-trained judge of human nature, she had blown it, and one gets pretty good at reading people working in a cocktail lounge. You see their eyes; in seconds you know their lines or their story in advance, and they never disappoint you. Everything she sensed about Michael told her that he could not be what he said he was.

But she had not told Ricky or Danny. That was new, too.

She had begun avoiding the group, and they knew it. Soon *she* would come under suspicion; paranoia was the fuel that kept the Stones in business. Perhaps the axe would fall as a result of her bringing Michael to what Ricky jokingly called his 'farm.' If the deal was somehow rotten, they would look back to her as the one who started it, and maybe *she* would wind up sinking to the bottom of the Gulf of Mexico. . . .

But then, hadn't she been 'ordered' to introduce Michael to the Stones in the first place? Yep. And if Ricky had any clue as to where she was driving right now, they'd really come after her with a gun in each hand.

Driving alone, she decided the whole mess had to be Providence. An ordered universe didn't allow such tangled cat's-cradles of facts to exist without a purpose.

She was unecessarily shaky when she opened up her apartment. No one was waiting inside.

It was a drab little dump, and this, too, was supposed to

change soon, but had not changed yet. All the furniture was used, had come from other owners who had discarded it. There was the ubiquitous television set that she hardly ever watched; its noise and flash, to her, was all sizzle with no steak.

She dumped her apron and bag on the bed. The bed sagged in the middle like a tarpaulin full of water.

The bathroom smelled of mildew and was in a permanent state of chaos thanks to her in-again, out-again style of living. Her medicine cabinet featured one of those mirrors that has somehow allowed green mould to edge between the glass and the silver; giving the whole thing the look of a slowly cataracting eye. There was the same kind of mysterious decay rimming the bathtub, seemingly doing just fine beneath paint and porcelain. She supposed normal housewives knew about such things, keeping their bathrooms operating-theatre clean, just like on television. But to Angie, television was not reality – she guessed that she was one of the few who really felt that way.

She spent rather too long in the shower, enjoying it as a kind of compensation for the mileage worn off her skin. She finally cranked the spray off when her hot water heater ran cold.

She fell asleep on the sagging bed, wrapped in a damp towel and reading a few pages of a paperback novel she had started three months ago and still not finished. *Have to catch up on my rea . . .* was her last thought before passing out.

Four hours later, she awoke with a snap from uneventful sleep, moved back into the muggy bathroom, and spent a careful half hour on her makeup. The red had faded from her eyes. She rebraided her hair and snugged into a tight pair of cutoffs, then threw on a billowing white Western-yoked work shirt with silver buttons and tied it off at her midriff. Oh yeah, she would turn heads on the street, alright, even in this basic getup.

Then she climbed back into her Mustang and drove to Mercy General Hospital.

She knew the route once inside the building. Three floors up, right out of the elevator, down the corridor past the nurses' station, four doors down, left into Room 326, hello.

Her pulse quickened as her car ate up the distance.

As she came abreast of Room 326 she heard voices, and stopped short of the door. She took a chance and casually walked past, as though looking for some other room. The people inside 326 did not notice her; traffic in the corridors was always heavy in the mornings.

The privacy curtain was drawn around the far bed inside the two-bed room, but as she passed the door, she saw shiny black shoes below the curtain, and recognized the voice of Father Carlos Laguna.

She leaned against the wall outside, trying to appear casual, checking her watch too many times, and tried her best to eavesdrop.

'The wages of sin are death,' pronounced Father Carlos Laguna.

'I know what the Bible says, Carlos,' Roberto Laguna said wearily. 'I've had it hammered into my skull; it's indelibly stamped.'

Roberto lay limp and uncaring in the embrace of an elevated, cradlelike hospital bed, his right arm in a heavy cast to the shoulder, suspended in a white canvas sling and hanging in midair like the arm of a construction crane. His right leg, also hit during the firefight at the Del Rio Ballroom, was in traction too. Intravenous leads snaked in and out of his good arm, and blackish bruises began to appear around the puncture points. The sterile, starched hospital sheets hurt his nose, the view from the window to the immediate right – a scenic panorama of the pipes and ducts lining the roof of another wing and admitting little daylight – hurt his eyes, and the bland hospital food insulted his fiery Spanish taste buds. The doctors insulted his intelligence. He wanted out from the moment he regained consciousness, and there was nothing he could do about it; this even helped to fan the flames of his anger higher.

And now his brother, the pious priest, was quoting the Bible at him. It became too much to bear.

He would have shrugged fatalistically, but he could not. The casts and braces restrained him. '*Mira mano*, if you want to talk to me, talk to me as a brother and not as a priest. I don't want to have to call you *Father*, Carlos.'

Father Carlos shrugged for his brother. 'I cannot separate the two, Roberto – no good Catholic can. Just as you cannot continue to live with a foot in each world.'

'I'm afraid I know what you're talking about,' Roberto said, having done the drill hundreds of times.

'I'm talking about church on Sunday for you, and business as usual on Monday . . . and don't patronize me.'

'Everyone else can balance the two,' said Roberto. 'Even priests do it.'

'Listen to me,' said Father Carlos. 'You can change the pattern. You're the youngest of us. You can leave this . . . this insanity behind you.'

'Can I leave my right arm behind me as well? Do you suggest I enter the priesthood? Carlos, I can't do that – cluck my tongue like an old woman and disapprove. I have to *fight*. Someone has to fight. It isn't you, and Miguel is gone.'

Father Carlos shook his head, sadly. Miguel's death had not been all that long ago.

'If we don't fight, we die, all of us. You think they'll stop at killing a priest once they get me out of the way? The *Corazones de Piedras* want to massacre the entire Laguna family, destroy the competition totally. So you *are* involved. You'd best be prepared.'

'I cannot.'

'But you can sit in church and talk about violence and death, and how sinful it is, and yet take no steps to stop it?'

'I am trying to stop it God's way, Roberto, not yours. Violence sows only more violence.'

'The Bible tells us so,' Roberto mocked. 'It's one thing to spout platitudes. It's another thing to drive down the street in Houston without wondering if they're behind you, or how you would fare if you were attacked at any instant. It's another thing when you have to wear a bulletproof vest as well as a tuxedo to your own sister's wedding, and to get

81

shot while sipping champagne. This is no different from the days of the *Revolución*. You keep talking about *me* changing, leaving it behind. What about our family? What about the Laguna name – do we leave it behind as well? Do I simply turn my back as they kill my brothers and sisters, and wait for my turn because I am a good little Catholic robot? I don't think so, my dear brother.'

Father Carlos moved to stare out the sliding hospital windows and the view, or rather, the absence of a view. He folded his hands behind his back.

'They are my brothers and sisters too,' he said gently, refusing to let his anger rise. Since they were both children, Roberto had always been able to get his dander up quickest. 'Because I refuse to shoot, and to kill for the Laguna name, that does not mean I have turned my back. I am *simpatico*. But I turn my back to violence. To sin, and death, I have turned my back.' Then he thought of his dealings with Michael Knight, something he could not yet discuss with Roberto, and added, 'But I am trying to deal with this terrible situation in my own way.'

'By praying for God's guidance, no doubt,' said Roberto. It was not an insult; they were beyond that.

'Yes, that too.' He turned for the door, touching Roberto briefly on the forehead. 'I must get to the church.'

'You're still my brother,' said Roberto. '*Vaya con Diós* . . . for all the good it will do.'

Father Carlos did not want to admit even to himself that he checked up and down the corridor twice for strangers looking like they might be armed before he stepped into the elevator.

As the doors slid smoothly shut, Angie stepped from her hiding place in the washroom of the visitors' lounge and made tracks for Room 326, Roberto's room. Assuring herself that there were no other visitors, she stepped in and closed the door behind her. No one noticed.

8

Devon unlatched the briefcase on the hotel bed and opened it. Michael stared down into two double rows of banded stacks of cash, five to a row, with the little oval portrait of Benjamin Franklin staring up toward him from each stack.

'Devon, you never cease to amaze me with your resources and connections,' he said, scratching his head. He'd barely had time to dress between Devon's early-morning phone call and his prompt arrival.

Devon eyed his charge dourly. 'You almost made me out to be a liar on this one. I recall telling you I had every contingency covered; that barely included this. Unlike you, I was up all night collecting this.'

'Robbing vending machines?'

Devon snapped the briefcase shut and twirled the silver latches. 'I've had no breakfast and bloody little sleep. Two hundred and forty thousand dollars –'

'Don't tell me. It's a lot of money to raise overnight. Somehow I sensed you were going to say that, Devon.' He smiled. 'Don't worry. It begins to look like I might pull it off. I bluffed them pretty successfully last night even though I was drenched in nervous sweat. You did your part; now I'll try to do mine.'

Devon would not let it go. 'I had to tap several different accounts to fill this order, Michael, and I think you should be aware that one of them was the Foundation's special account for the Charity Benefit Fund.'

'Whoops. Muscular dystrophy, Special Olympics, that sort of thing?'

Devon nodded.

'I'll be careful.' He whipped the damp towel from around his neck and pulled a fresh shirt out of the hotel closet.

'Please do.' Devon was digging in his suit pocket for something. He drew out an elongated pad and offered Michael a gold pen.

'What is this?'

Devon's eyebrows went up in innocence. 'Why, a receipt for the money, of course.'

'I'm supposed to sign a receipt?' Michael was suddenly unsure whether he was awake.

'It's just a formality,' Devon added, as though that explained anything.

'You think I'm going to run off to the Bahamas with this or something?' He waited a beat, then added: 'And leave my car behind?'

Devon's brows went up again. '*Your* car?'

'Oh, just give me the damned thing, Devon.' He peered briefly at the receipt book, and resignedly put his signature on the dotted line.

Devon separated the copies and handed Michael a sheet of pink flimsy. He checked the signature. 'Very good,' he said, dryly. 'I can actually read it. You *are* improving.' *Zip!* – the receipt vanished into Devon's coat pocket. 'Now why don't you order us both some breakfast?'

'Hey, wait a minute,' said Michael. 'I haven't counted this yet.'

'Trust me,' Devon said.

'Sure thing,' Michael shot back, lifting the briefcase, absently testing its weight, then replacing it. 'As far as you trusted me, right?'

84

'But I *do* trust you, Michael, after my own fashion.' Devon seated himself in one of the chairs next to the front window of the room. These places all look alike, Michael thought – there's always a little round table and two chairs by the window. They always give you a room with two beds when you're by yourself. 'Now that we've dealt with that,' continued Devon, 'I'd like eggs Benedict with crumpets, not toast, and make sure they're hot. Extra butter, not margarine.'

'You mean we don't discuss this any more?' said Michael still disoriented.

Devon smiled and laced his tapered fingers behind his head. 'Black coffee,' he said.

Michael blew out a breath and picked up the phone to punch in the room service number. 'You're buying, smart guy,' he said in a tone of mock revenge.

The room service at the Houston Plaza was surprisingly good, and probably monstrously expensive, Michael signed the tab without looking at the amount. If there was going to be some screw-up while all the money was in his official possession, he wanted to enjoy his last meal.

Devon ate with gusto, obviously hungry, putting away whole cups of coffee between sentences. Michael picked desultorily at his fluffy scrambled eggs and eight rashers of bacon – mostly he sat and nibbled at the bacon, which was crisp and tasty. He fiddled with the tiny tubs of jelly and cream, accidentally dumping too much of the latter into his coffee. It sat untouched, too cold to drink now.

'Anything to report on KITT?' Devon was apparently making what he considered to be chitchat. He had probably been in radio contact with the Knight Industries Two Thousand all morning; had most likely parked next to it in the Plaza lot.

'KITT's okay. His Spanish is improving.' He sipped the cold coffee and grimaced. 'By the way, I had him log and run makes on the cars we found at Ricky's ranch party last night.'

'And?'

'Intriguing collection of people. Several from Florida, Seattle, Tucson, Canada . . . as far away as Peru and as near as right here in Houston.'

'Hm. Mostly ports of entry in to the United States,' Devon noted.

Michael wondered idly if the fabulous Roxy was some kind of smuggler.

'It also shores up the indication that the Stones are nomadic,' said Devon. 'No permanent addresses, no families, no roots. They'll rent a house or apartment or business, stay a week or two, then sublet it as a drop point, or just vanish. Their enormous cash flow allows that kind of freedom. They've certainly brought guerilla warfare tactics and big business together on home ground.' He stopped just short of mopping his plate with a bite of leftover crumpet, and crossed the knife and fork out of habit.

'The Lagunas are sitting ducks,' said Michael. 'So much for established, small-town owner-operated business.' He poked at his eggs with his fork and said, 'So if the operation comes off and we get the Stones out of the Lagunas' hair, what happens then? Business as usual, guns-across-the-border, and all of that?'

'We've already discussed it, Michael.'

'Yeah, you're right.' He was rubbing salt in his own wounds unnecessarily. He just wanted to get it all over with and see what was left that was worthwhile, in the aftermath. There had to be something of ethical value.

'When will you know if it's on? The deal, I mean.'

'If my phone rings and it's Angie calling, that means we have a buy.' He noticed that he kept glancing toward the phone, and that every time he did something jumped inside his chest.

'Since it seems imminent, I have to tell you some things that may seem unnecessarily redundant,' said Devon, pushing back from the table and finishing his coffee.

'Like the serial numbers on the bills are all a matter of record?'

'Yes, that, and the fact that the handle of the briefcase has a homer sewn into it. You'll be able to track it on KITT's monitors up to a distance of several miles with no obstructions. Just in case.'

'The handle – that's pretty good. That's what cocaine smugglers use when they're running dope back into the U.S. It never occurs to the customs guys to check the handle when they're so busy checking the case – and a little handle can hold an awfully expensive taste.'

'Notify me – have KITT send a signal – as soon as the buy goes through. Stick with the money. I can have the weapons picked up at the drop point, then we can trace them back to wherever they were stolen from.'

'Got it,' said Michael. To change the subject, he asked, 'You bring your Bentley?'

'Yes,' said Devon with obvious pride. 'Since it's just out of the Knight shop I thought I'd see what it would do on these long, flat, straightaways.'

One of Devon's passions – recently revealed to Michael – was antique automobiles. It seemed fitting that someone behind the development of a super car like KITT would also maintain a peculiar reverence for the older classics of the automotive industry. The pride of Devon's collection was a supercharged 1937 Bentley, though his other acquisitions ran the time gamut from 1920s Cadillacs to a 1952 Nash-Healy, recently bought from a retired Treasury agent.

'In fact, I thought the old girl needed a run in the desert air,' said Devon fondly. 'That's the –'

He was cut off, because they were both staring at the telephone, which was ringing at last.

Angie was sunk into KITT's passenger seat again crossing and uncrossing her long, perfect legs in a gesture Michael recognized as indicative of her unease. She was looking quite well, done up casually in a knotted white cowboy shirt and cutoff denim shorts. The glaring whiteness of the shirt and the abbreviation of the shorts all emphasized her even tan, and she proved to be as easy on Michael's eyes this morning as she had been the previous night.

The briefcase was in the back seat, and Michael had an

even harder time keeping his eyes off that. He continually spot-checked the rearview mirror to reassure himself it had not blown away, or disintegrated, or . . . something.

They were headed out of town in the general direction of the ranch. Angie smoked.

'Where to?' said Michael.

'Just keep going this way,' she said. 'Till I tell you to turn.' She pointed down the road with her cigarette. There was desert and a lot of nothing ahead.

'We meeting them at the house?'

'No.' She continued not to look at him. 'Look. I'm sorry about the way I treated you last night. Sorry for you getting slapped around, too.'

'All in a day's work. But thanks, just the same. I didn't know how you felt; whether you approved of that kind of action or not.'

'You seem pretty different from Ricky and D.D.,' she said.

'Not like the run of the mill, for this business?'

'Yeah. Not at all.'

'All camouflage,' Michael said convincingly. 'But I was about to say the same thing about you.'

She seemed more at ease then, and settled down to watch the countryside fly by. They were entering a raw outland of scrub and cactus, similar to where Michael had test-fired the American 180. It was a lot less attractive in the daylight.

'There's a rural fork about nine miles ahead. The sign'll say "Crombie's Gas and Cold Beer."'

'Sounds good to me,' Michael said. 'Is that the, uh, you know – "last chance for gas before Waco" stop, or something?'

'Something like that.' She butted one cigarette and immediately lit another.

When they hit the fork, the highway narrowed to a single blacktopped lane with a wide shoulder for passing. Obviously, not much traffic came this way. It was a route that was once important for something, but which had been bypassed when Texas's highway system was revamped in the 1950s and 1960s. Heat pounded down and threw glassy shimmer patterns up from the pavement, along with those hallucinatory pools of water in the road that seem endemic to the desert.

'Turn left up here,' said Angie. 'On that little road.'

'Far enough away from civilization for these guys, to be sure,' said Michael, as he watched the road turn to hard-packed dirt beneath KITT's wheels. He pushed the air conditioning in the cabin of the car up another notch. 'Uh – Angie?'

'Yeah?' she said, between puffs. She was perspiring, and not from the heat.

'I hope the Stones are professional enough to realize that I'm not stupid enough to wander out into the middle of the desert with a briefcase full of loot without backup and a contingency plan . . .?' Actually, Michael's 'plan' consisted only of the radio fix KITT could offer Devon, and the homing beeper secreted in the handle of the briefcase. 'I mean, I don't want to get killed any more than you or anybody else does. A nice, simple exchange between businessmen, that's what I want. And nothing else – no extras, no frills, and no surprises. They *do* understand that, don't they?' He kept his eyes on the road. It was getting hilly again, with twists and turns that obscured the nature of the oncoming miles.

'Uh – I guess so,' said Angie uncertainly. 'I'm sure they wouldn't try to double-cross you, I mean.'

'Glad to hear it. Then why are you so agitated?'

'That's easy. I hate guns.'

It was plausible. Not having one had kept Michael out of trouble twice now. But today he could not risk going into the buy situation totally uncovered – and so he had hidden, in a flip-up compartment beneath the back seat – right under the briefcase, in fact – a fully loaded American 180, one of the samples Devon had exhibited inside the Knight Industries truck. Even if the Stones found it, he could claim it was the copy he'd brought out of El Salvador, according to his story of the night before.

'I'm not too fond of guns myself,' he said.

Another sign bumped past to the right: Only Five More

Miles to Crombie's *'Ice Cold' Beer and Gas*!

Michael laughed. 'I wonder if that means the gas is ice cold, or the beer is some kind of bogus cold – ?'

'Those signs have been standing up since the Forties, at least,' Angie said. 'It's a wonder a dust-devil hasn't blown them away.'

'You know this place, then?'

'I've been here once or twice.'

He did not have to much time to wonder what *that* meant.

Poking up out of the sand around a wide, looping curve in the road was a ramshackle old joint that appeared to be Crombie's. It seemed to grow more decrepit as they got closer; two ancient gas pumps with opaque white globes stood in front like antique robots, guarding a creaking clapboard structure covered with rusted Coca-Cola signs and blistered paint. There was a single garage bay, its contents hidden by a wooden roll-door that was down and secured by a padlock that had been factory-fresh during the First World War. What office windows weren't broken were either obscured by drifts of white sand or shaded behind a crazy-quilt pattern of old motor-oil signs, some brands dating from the 1940s, as Angie had indicated.

'I take it that Crombie's is no longer a going concern,' said Michael, caution creeping into his tone. He slowed as they drew closer in the car.

Angie checked her wristwatch. 'It's been shut down a long time,' she said simply. 'The Stones occasionally use it as a drop.'

'I don't see any trucks,' he said. 'I thought they were going to supply transport for the guns.'

'It's probably locked in the garage. Don't let the appearance of the door padlock fool you.' From her shoulder bag – more properly a saddlebag with a broad strap of cowhide – she withdrew a silver key. 'This fits it.'

'I don't like this,' said Michael. 'No people.'

'They're waiting inside, away from the windows.'

Michael looked at her.

'Well, that's what they told *me*,' she finished.

Michael brought KITT to a stop on the road, avoiding

actually turning in to where the gas station's drive once had been. As unobtrusively as possible, he punched KITT's SURVEILLANCE MODE bar.

'What's that?'

'Computerized auto alarm. A habit. I told you about the gadgets,' he said, climbing out and reaching into the back seat. After a moment of hesitation, he pulled the American 180 from its hiding place and laid it, safety off, across the seat.

'Oh my God,' Angie said, paling.

'You know how to use this thing?'

'I haven't the faintest idea,' she said. 'Just the way it looks scares the water out of me.'

'Not a good idea in the desert,' he smiled. 'It's just for backup; a little safety valve of my own – don't worry, okay?'

'Let's just go down there and get this over with.' She hugged her arms together.

Michael came up from the back seat with the briefcase. He looked up into the sky. 'I thought I heard something . . . strange.' He peered westward.

Coming from the direction of the blazing mid-afternoon sun was the machine-gun whir of helicopter rotor blades. Michael could see no aircraft; the glare of the sun blotted out everything.

Angie walked past the verge where gas price signs had once stood, past the twin gas pumps, empty and rusting, and fit her silver key into the lock on the garage door. It popped obediently open.

'They're coming in by chopper?' said Michael. 'Looks just like what I've heard of the Stones, for them to fly in right out of the sun. That's a warfare tactic for sure!'

'It is a war, Michael,' she said, softly.

When he turned to look at her he saw the American 180, its safety still off, in her hands . . . and the red dot of the laser beam sight hovering right next to his heart.

'What you have to do now,' she said slowly and clearly, 'is put that briefcase down, right on the ground – right where 'ya sit, as they say in Texas.'

Michael warily placed the briefcase at his feet. 'Is this the way the Stones do business?'

She appeared to ponder that. 'No. The Stones would splatter you all over the side of your car and leave you for the coyotes to eat.'

Michael's heart hammered. This was how he had almost had his ticket punched permanently the first time, only the desert was in Reno, Nevada. Everything else was the same; a rat-trap double cross, a good guy who turned out to be a bad guy who turned out to be a beautiful woman with a gun in her hand. The last time, Michael had literally got his face blown off and he was alive only because Wilton Knight came along to save his hide. This time, his mind raced ahead, Wilton Knight was dead. He thought fleetingly of jumping to try to get back into KITT, inside the protection of his bulletproof skin . . . but Angie had obviously been lying about knowing how to use the gun. He remembered the statistics of the American 180, and quickly calculated that by the time he would be in a position to close KITT's door there would be – roughly – seventy bullets in him. No contest. His hand left the handle of the briefcase.

The helicopter emerged from the searing yellow disc of the sun and roared over their heads like a smug bird of prey.

'Now what?' he said, dully.

She swallowed, but the gun did not waver. 'I'm not going to kill you,' she said. 'Now you walk toward the garage. Five paces ahead of me.' She was too smart to allow him to lead her close enough to disarm her with a well-timed rearward kick.

She picked up the briefcase, balanced the American 180 in the other hand. That might have been the time for a fast move, but now Michael stood too far away.

The chopper circled above them and hovered above an area behind the service station. Wisps of dust floated, then began to whip around in miniature hurricane patterns as the machine settled toward the earth with a horrendous eggbeater racket. Sound carried very well in the middle of the desert, and that was the only sound there was.

Michael stood in the doorway of the garage. 'Aren't you forgetting my contingency plan?' he said to Angie, somewhat futilely.

'I'm sorry, Michael.'

The *whup-whup* of the rotors slowed. The chopper was on the ground.

'Now please step inside or I'll have to shoot.'

Arms up, Michael retreated into the dusty darkness of the enclosed garage. The light was sliced completely off when Angie slid the door shut, and he had to blink to adjust his eyes in the new dark.

He heard the padlock click into place. Retreating footsteps blended with and were blanked out by the noise of the chopper.

'KITT,' he said into his comlink. 'You still with me, buddy?'

'What do you plan to do, Michael? She's just entered the helicopter.'

'Good question,' he said, mostly to himself. He could command KITT to ram the damned thing before it took off . . . but that would involve jeopardy to human life, which was contrary to KITT's specific programming. They might shoot; the gas tank of the helicopter might blow on impact and fry both them *and* the cash. And what good would stopping them in the desert do? They were armed and Michael was not. They'd kill him for sure, and long before KITT could do anything about it.

'You reading the homer?'

'Loud and clear at one blip per second.'

'As soon as that chopper leaves the ground I want you to get in here,' he said. 'I'll stand back against the eastern wall. But hurry!'

He had a second to bitterly reflect that once he *had* brought a gun along for protection, it had got him into hot water. He had lost not only the money, but one of Devon's special-requisition machine guns. It didn't make any difference – if this was the plan, Angie probably had a .32 tucked away in her saddle-bag purse that would have served the cause. And she was probably an excellent shot – it had been sheer stupidity to think anybody connected to the Stones would not have a lot of hands-on experience with firearms.

But he had begun to like her, even within the limits of their brief relationship. He had thought she honestly found Ricky and D.D. to be pretty repulsive.

He had been wrong, that was all.

Outside, the chopper blades came back up to running speed. Michael heard KITT's unique turbine revving, and braced himself against the far wall of the garage.

The rickety wooden building shuddered as the chopper lifted off.

An instant later, KITT's black prow split the rolling door in two, rendering most of it into hurtling pieces of kindling. Broken boards clattered across the concrete floor and what seemed like a hundred pounds of dust, shaken loose from every old nook in the building, sifted down in a brown cloud.

Michael jumped to the driver's side door before the dust could suffocate him. KITT's coolers were still blowing. The safe, air-conditioned, bulletproof sanctuary of KITT's cabin was exactly where Michael wanted to be at this moment.

'KITT, we've got to catch the copter! Can you ground-track at helicopter speed?' With the homer providing a beacon, it might not be impossible.

'*I'll do my best, Michael,*' said KITT as his rear wheels spun to dig them out of the debris of the demolished garage door.

As they shot backward, Michael saw the silhouette of a Bell two-seater helicopter duck down beyond a hill to the west. They were deliberately avoiding following the path of the desert trail, as though they had read Michael's plan. He hit the monitor button and was provided with an overplay map of the surrounding area with the chopper's homer a bright red blip and KITT a small circle with black crosshairs. The whirlybird was moving away fast.

'KITT, are we too far away to use the microwave jammers?' His fingers played across the board, punching KITT into the bright blue AUTO PURSUIT mode so he could concentrate on what he was doing.

Two indicators popped on at once: SURFACE-TO-AIR SURVEILLANCE and MICROWAVE JAMMERS.

'The idea is feasible, Michael, but we've got to gain more distance on them for it to be effective.'

'Do it! Give it all the juice you've got!'

The red digital speedometer blurred from sixty to eighty-five. KITT's sophisticated suspension would take care of the bumps as far as potential damage on this dirt switchback was concerned, but for Michael it was like riding in a roller-coaster car with a few loose bolts securing the wheels.

'Faster!'

They were approaching foothills; mountains rose up in the distance and the trail began to incline.

'Michael?'

'Yes?' he shouted through clenched teeth, to keep from biting his tongue as they valleyed-out in the ditches.

'She's got Devon's money, doesn't she?'

'Yeah!' Even though the car was steering itself, he hung onto the wheel. 'KITT, give me whatever you've got on the Foundation's Charity Benefit Fund!'

Data began to roll up on the other monitor screen, but the car was jigging so wildly that Michael could not focus on the glowing dot-matrix lettering.

'Skip the readout!' he shouted. 'Just give me the gist of it!'

Crunch! – KITT went briefly airborne himself as they came out of a deep, stomach-lurching rut in the road.

'Michael,' KITT continued in utter, machine calm, as though the forces of gravity and inertia had no effect on his voice – which they did not. *'Do you know who the Foundation's Charity Benefit Fund is for – ?'*

'Don't tell me – orphans . . .'

'And widows.'

Michael would have winced, but his face was already locked in a grimace. 'How are we doing?'

'The helicopter is climbing, but we're proportionately closer to it. My jammers are already drawing off power from their coil.'

'Don't shut the engine off; just slow it down!' Michael

doubted whether they were even close enough to do the former anyway.

The ascent of the helicopter slowed. It continued climbing, but less vigorously, like a dopey wasp trying to get a clear fix on its nest. The engine began to skip and miss under the bombardment from KITT's jammers.

Michael witnessed the whole thing with enthusiasm. 'Give it all you've got! Pull enough juice out of her coil to set her down and you get a monument in the Automobile Hall of Fame!'

KITT kept barrelling up the narrow pass, headed into the mountainous terrain, drawing ever closer to the underbelly of the Bell chopper. A broad brown plume of tailwind dust marked their progress into the hills.

The helicopter dipped precariously toward the car, losing spunk. Michael's eyes locked on it. A rusting sign with shotgun pellet dents obscuring its aged message flashed past on the right too fast to read.

With KITT still in AUTO PURSUIT, Michael keyed open the sunroof. They were beneath the chopper now, sucking it magnetically down. The skids hovered some twenty feet above KITT's roof, and Michael began to climb out of the moving car.

KITT was speaking again, but Michael could not hear because of the wind drag whipping his hair backwards as the copter and the car slowly married positions.

A little closer, he thought. A matter of yards now.

KITT's rear wheels locked and the car nosed into a forward skid as full braking power was engaged. A roiling thundercloud of smoke and dust enveloped the car, and Michael was nearly pitched headfirst out of the sunroof opening, to plummet into the abyss he saw below.

With a stomach-wrenching *clunk*! KITT's front wheels fell atop a crumbling miniature avalanche of sunbaked dirt clods and white caliche rock. The debris rolled downward for at least fifty feet and came to rest in a long-dry, deeply-cut desert riverbed, scattering noisily about. KITT's last-second retro-rocket blast had saved them from somersaulting into the gorge below and landing on their roof.

Hanging out of the sunroof hatch, Michael impotently watched the Bell helicopter regain strength with distance, climb, and clear the mountain above them. He slammed his fist into KITT's roof in frustration, then slid back down into the cabin.

'*I'm sorry, Michael,*' said KITT. '*I attempted to warn you.*'

'S'okay. Nobody's fault.' Their front end was still jutting off the cliff edge.

'*Brace for retro-thrust,*' said KITT, getting back to business while Michael was still shaking.

'Yeah.'

With a heavy whoosh of air compression – the reverse application of KITT's turbo-boost function – the car shot backward into the air and landed on all four wheels.

'That must be what the sign back there was about,' said Michael. 'This road hasn't been used for years, and one of the reasons is that it terminates in a dry riverbed. That's just outstanding.'

He watched the crimson blip do a slow fade on KITT's Number One monitor screen. It finally became inaudible.

'Damn!' he said, smacking the dashboard, pulling his punch at the last minute to avoid hitting any unexpected buttons.

'*I've lost them on physical tracking and radar as well,*' KITT put in unnecessarily.

'Quiet. I've got to think up another plan.'

'*Widows and orphans, Michael.*'

His eyes jumped to the vox-box mounted above the steering column, and he felt a flush of embarrassment.

'KITT?'

'*Yes, Michael?*'

He made him wait for it. 'No monument,' he said.

9

Father Carlos was seated in one of the front pews of the vast church where Michael had first encountered him. His shoulders were slumped, and he looked very much like a defeated man.

'I don't know anything about her,' he said slowly, not meeting the eyes of his visitor.

'You gave me her name!' Michael exploded, not caring that his voice echoed throughout the church and distracted the endless parade of old women and unemployed workers who stopped by at the midday hour to worship. He thought that for the first time in his life, he was close to striking a man of the cloth – but one who permitted the tango of illegal arms sales to go on in his own hometown, a man who had allowed his own backyard to become desecrated. There was not much beyond contempt in Michael's mind for a man like Father Carlos . . . that and smouldering anger.

'Her name was given to me,' the priest said in a crushed tone.

'By whom?' Michael pressed.

'I can't tell you.'

Father Carlos's answer almost died away with Michael's last vestiges of composure. In a voice of deadly softness, looking away, toward the altar, Michael said, 'You can tell me, *Father*, and you will, because your sordid little gunrunning racket got me into this mess, and now Angie has flown the coop with two hundred and forty thousand of *my* dollars. None of the Lagunas are worth two hundred and forty K to me; you'd best remember that . . . because there aren't too many of you left.' He spun and bore down on the priest. 'Do you *read* me, *Father*? Do you understand now?'

Father Carlos looked up then, his eyes red-rimmed. 'Please try to understand, Michael,' he said. 'The name was given to me in the sanctity of the confessional. If I told you I'd violate my vow of privacy.'

Michael stuck his hands into his rear pockets, waiting out the explanation. There was not much more to it; Father Carlos was at least sticking by his faith.

Suddenly his anger was gone. It left his body like a physical yoke lifting from his shoulders, with a single breath blown out in a sigh. 'You mean I have to win fair and square?' he said after a moment.

Father Carlos's response surprised him: 'My brother Roberto has disappeared.'

'Disap – ?' This was a new factor in the equation. 'I thought he was in the hospital, in Mercy General. Disappeared where?'

'He left a few hours ago, against advice from the doctors. He hardly even resorted to the formality of checking out. It's a Friday – Mercy General is very busy. I'm sure he was able to leave unencumbered. He left – if he *did* leave of his own will – without a word, and no one has heard from him since this morning. I have no clues as to where he might have gone.'

'Do you think the Stones are behind it?'

'I don't know what else to think, given the circumstances . . . do you?'

'At least that gives me the hospital.'

Father Carlos paused in confusion. 'I don't understand what you mean.'

100

An idea was percolating in Michael's head. As a lead, it was not worth much, but it could lead to greater things. 'That gives me the hospital as a place to start. Roberto may be many things, but he's not crazy enough to leave for no reason, right?'

'Of course not.'

'Then it follows that Roberto, my dear Father Carlos, is sane. And when sane people run – or are chased – they always leave tracks. Always.'

'*Now* I think I read you,' said the priest with a sly little smile.

'I'll let you know what happens,' Michael said, as he turned to rush out. He stopped. 'And, uh – sorry about that little outburst, before.'

'Don't worry.' Father Carlos patted his shoulder. 'Forgiving is my business.'

The sleek black street machine flashed down one of Houston's main drags on a beeline course for Mercy General Hospital.

Michael kept the windows up and the air conditioning on maximum. 'KITT, has the Department of Motor Vehicles computer come up with anything on Angie's Mustang?'

Readout played on the monitor screens as KITT recited the information: '*Full name, Angeline Beth Martin, Texas driver's licence number F-10726-B, filed at the DMV here in Houston. Her licence expires next April. Current address: 20362-C Big Rock Road. . . .*'

'That's the apartment,' said Michael. 'Forget that; the car's not even there. Probably out at the Stone's ranch house – if anybody's still *there*, either.'

'*Continuing . . . Father: Stafford Martin II, deceased as of 2 March 1978. Mother: Elaine ("Lainy") Waldrop, no record of marriage . . . whereabouts unknown.*'

Michael slowed down for a yellow light to let some jump-the-gun pedestrian cross. Apparently, nobody in Houston waited for anything, including traffic lights. Michael was the only driver who stopped for the light.

'We're batting a million so far,' muttered Michael. 'What

about siblings?'

'*An older sister, Monica Johnson, divorced. Angie Martin used Monica's address for a mail drop until two months ago.*'

'Is she missing in action, too?'

'*I have an address listed in Waco, Texas.*'

'We don't need that right now. Let's see if we can get a line on old Roberto.' Michael turned into Mercy General's visitors' parking lot.

Michael moved through the maze of lobby, elevator, and corridor, and when he arrived at Room 326 he found it being aired. Linens were in heaps on the floor. There were no patients in occupancy.

'Uh – can I help you?'

A nurse was peeking around the doorframe. She looked Michael up and down as though he were a lost little boy.

'This was Roberto Laguna's room, right?'

'That's partially correct,' the nurse said with a bemused smile. 'Mr Laguna checked out this morning. And visiting hours are just wrapping up. And –' she was ticking the items off on her fingers '– you breezed right past the nurses' station like a high-speed zombie. I tried to flag you down but your eyes were . . . sort of fixed straight ahead.'

'I was hoping he might still be here. *Checked* out, did you say?'

'Officially and completely,' she said. She stepped into the room with him, allowing Michael a thorough look. Her nametag read *Barry Watson, R.N.*, and she looked to be a healthly and trim thirty-five or so. Her auburn hair was pinned up; wisps of it escaped to make a stylish kind of corona around her face. She had a ready smile and an open manner. Michael found her attractive.

He pointed at the badge. 'Barry? Is that for real?'

'You want to see my birth certificate?'

He laughed. 'I believe you. Anything else you can tell me about –'

'About Mr Laguna? No,' she replied. 'Routine checkout. I was on duty this morning, so I saw him. I'm pulling double shifts so I can get the weekend off through Monday. I just came back on.' She folded her arms, leaned easily against the wall inside the door, and said, 'You know, I don't know who you are, and I'm really not authorized to be answering questions like this . . .'

'This could be a matter of life and death,' said Michael, trying to sound earnest and not like he was invoking a cliché to get past her. 'He wasn't supposed to leave. His brother told me the doctors advised against it, and nobody knew he was gone until he *was* gone.' He moved nearer. 'Barry, I'd really love it if I didn't have to squeeze past all the protocol with Admissions, downstairs, you know what I mean?'

The corners of her mouth turned up. 'Don't beg,' she said, almost laughing. 'I'm not the Big Bad Maternal Nurse. What do you need to know?'

'Well, first of all –'

'Wait a minute,' she said, cutting him off. 'For every one of yours you have to answer one of mine. Fair deal?'

Michael found himself being charmed. 'Sure.'

'Then shoot.'

'Oh, no,' he said, playing along even though he knew there was little time to spare. 'After you.'

'All right. What's your name, stranger?' She was clearly relishing this impromptu flirtation.

'Michael Knight, and yes, it's my real name.'

'I like Michael.'

'Anything odd about Roberto's checkout? Did he have some kind of escort, or were there any goons helping him with his luggage, anything like that?'

'That's two questions,' cautioned Barry. 'No goons. His girlfriend was with him. I guess it was his girlfriend. She helped him out. And speaking of girlfriends, are you tied to one right now?'

'Not especially. What did she –'

'Uh-uh, wait a second. Whose life and death might this be a matter of?'

He cleared his throat nervously. 'Er – mine, among many others. Possibly tonight.'

She pursed her fine lips; nodded. 'Next question?'

'Could you identify a photo of the girl if I showed you

one?'

'Maybe. But it might cost you.'

'What, for example.'

She had thought it out in advance. 'For example, how about dinner? Assuming, of course, that you live through the night?'

'Barry, I'd like nothing better. Provided I live and you can identify the picture, it's a date. It'd be the first thing I found in Houston that I liked.'

'I'll take that as a compliment. But it's not a date. It's just a dinner. We'll see if it develops into anything else, hm?' She waited for a response and, getting none, said, 'Well? Do you have the picture?'

'It's in my car. Can you – ?'

'Sneaky boy,' she said. 'I have to watch out for these younger men. Always pulling stuff like asking me to come to their cars so I can see their etchings, that sort of thing.' She peered back out into the hallway.

'I'm serious – the picture's in my car.'

She nodded. 'Okay. I'll assume you're not fibbing, and I'll make an excuse and be down in five minutes. How's that?'

'Superlative. Thanks . . . Barry.' He gave her a smile and a quick kiss on the cheek as he walked out. She smelled faintly of jasmine.

'Welcome to Houston,' he said wonderingly, as he walked back to the elevators.

Waiting for Barry in the lobby struck Michael as being oddly similar to his first meeting with Angie. She had waited for him in the lobby of the Plaza in about the same way, and after knowing him for about as long.

His mind was racing ahead. Was it possible the woman who had left with Roberto was Angie? That he had taken her someplace secure – or vice versa, she had taken him, because of his wounds, which had been pretty severe – then stopped to freshen up just long enough to make the meeting with Michael outside the Embers? Angie was apparently not only a crack shot with ultra-sophisticated military

104

weaponry, but a pretty good actress as well.

And then there were Ricky and D.D. and the other Stones. Had she taken Roberto to them (if it *was* Angie)? Had she taken the money and split, double-crossing both Michael *and* the Stones? If the Stones had been stranded at some meeting place with a truckload of illegal guns while Michael was busy chasing a helicopter in another part of the state, they were apt to be a bit peeved by this late hour.

Across the hospital lobby the elevator chime gonged softly and Barry squeezed between the opening steel doors. From what Michael could see of her legs, between the modest hem of the starched, white uniform and the large, clunky crepe-soled work shoes, they were quite nice.

'I've only got a minute,' she said, breathlessly, as she caught up to him.

'The car's right outside,' he said, lightly taking her forearm to hurry her along. Damn! The sun was setting already. He'd nearly lost an entire day!

He opened KITT's driver's-side door for her. 'Go ahead.'

She did not realize what he meant until she looked in and saw the Super Dash light up in all its multicoloured, graphically complex splendour. KITT loved to show off.

'What kind of rig is *this*?' she said, half in curiosity and half in awe.

'KITT, give me a visual on Angie. Put the driver's licence shot and the tape freeze-frame side-by-side.'

Both video monitors lit up, the right one displaying the driver's mug shot, the left, a random head and shoulders view of Angie recorded while she had been sitting in the passenger seat.

'That's . . . really amazing,' Barry said in a diminished voice.

'Is that the woman? The girlfriend?'

'I'm pretty certain it is. She had her hair tied back in a braid just like that. You see a lot of faces in the hospital, and you don't remember a lot of them, but I remember that girl and her hair, alright.' She waited a beat, then said, 'She's not my competition, is she?'

'No way, Barry – I prefer people safe, like you.'

She got out of the car and wrapped her arms around his neck. 'Then go do your mission.' She kissed him full on the mouth. 'That's for luck. Now I gotta get back to work. Take care.' And she was off.

'You, too,' he managed to say.

Barry had verified that Angie and Roberto had left the hospital together. What had happened with Roberto in the time between then and her meeting with Michael? Why would Roberto Laguna so willingly tag along with somebody that his own brother knew to be an insider with the Stones, their mortal enemies?

'Devon is calling in, Michael,' said KITT once Barry was out of earshot.

'Tell him you're still parked and waiting for me to come out,' said Michael. 'I need some time to piece this all together, Don't lie, just –'

'I'm afraid I know – tell the truth selectively.'

'You've got it.'

Michael seated himself in the car. 'Give me the rest of the fetch on Angeline Martin,' he said. 'Go back and start with her sister's address in Waco.'

'New information in on the DMV computer,' said KITT. *'Monica Johnson no longer lives in Waco, but in Gatesville, thirty-nine miles to the west-southwest.'*

'You have an updated street address?'

'3430 Daystar Way, Apartment number 12.'

'Cross-reference Roberto Laguna. They might have left in his car; it isn't accounted for either.' Unless Roberto got led into a trap and the car was disposed of, Michael's mind suggested.

'Lime-green 1977 Pontiac Firebird, Texas plate number 375 RKJ. Roberto Bavas Laguna, licence number –'

'Put a hold on that,' Michael interrupted. 'Plot us a fast course to Gatesville.'

'Si, señor.'

'And stop being a wiseacre, motor mouth.'

10

Gatesville was the archetype of the sun-washed, sleepy little backwater Western town, a burg with a couple of gas stations and diners to its name as the main attractions, and a main street that was actually called Main Street. The town's traffic lights became yellow blinkers after six p.m., and the local constabulary was a division of the sheriff's bureau that policed Gatesville and its neighbouring towns along the highway string all at once. It was almost a 'bedroom community,' border-to-border with another yawny nothing-happening place just like itself.

When KITT's contoured ebony form cruised slowly down the main street, all the regulars at the drugstore lunch counter took notice, and the origin of the black car was a topic of idle speculation throughout the following week. This was a town where no two cars were alike anyway, and everyone was more or less identified by their 'wheels.' In this proverbial small town, Michael stuck out like the proverbial sore thumb, feeling more ill at ease here than even in Houston.

'Hell, we could sweep this whole place end-to-end in

about forty-five minutes,' said Michael, watching his own progress on an overlay map of Gatesville displayed on KITT's monitor.

'I'm scanning for either licence plate number,' said KITT.

'Keep an eye out for rental cars, too. A town like this has almost no need for them.'

'Shouldn't we proceed directly to Monica Johnson's apartment?'

'Not yet. Stop up here.'

KITT pulled up in front of a liquor store, where Michael got out to consult the yellow pages tacked to a phone booth. The Gatesville phone directory covered seven other towns just like it to the north and east, and still was barely the thickness of a magazine. Inside the liquor store the counterman peered out from between a couple of sun-faded Black Label paste-ups.

Kind of creepy, Michael thought. Everyone always watching everyone else, to get gossip, perhaps. He was a confirmed urbanite; he harboured no misty-eyed nostalgia for the homey illusion of 'small-town America' that was purely the province of television commercials, and not reality. Just getting out of the car in such a place, and feeling the weight of dozens of unseen eyes settle on him, made Michael uncomfortable. Out here, everyone tipped their hat, knew everyone else, was friendly and cordial, almost formal . . . but every one of them had a loaded gun stashed in their house somewhere.

He quickly found what he was looking for: MOTELS.

'There's only a couple of places listed,' he said as he climbed back into the car. 'I'm gambling that Angie might have led them here, but maybe they saw the motels on the way in – or out – and decided to lay over for a while, let the heat go in other directions, before they hit up her sister. Since she was using Monica's apartment as a mail drop when she knew the Stones, if Angie has double-crossed the Stones as well as us it makes more sense *not* to visit her sister.'

'I don't think I follow that, Michael.'

'Don't worry, KITT. I've got one of my hunches.'

'Like the hunch that got us stranded in –'

'Quiet. Make for the feeder roads. It'll only take a few minutes to actually check out the few motels there are around here . . . and there aren't any *ho*tels.'

They got under way. Everybody noticed.

'I hate to bring this up, Michael, but I'm still registering an urgent call signal from –'

'From Devon, I know,' he said. 'Tell him you don't know where I am. But that things look good.'

'Michael, I feel compelled to point out that despite my understanding of how you function, I am still not constitutionally constructed to lie.'

'Look, KITT. Use your impeccable machine logic. If I talk to Devon, the first thing he'll ask about is the money. I don't have the money; Angie has it. And we may have Angie in a few minutes. See?'

'I'm afraid not.'

'Well,' he said as the road broadened to rural-highway width and they approached the first of the roadside mom-and-pop motels listed in the phone book, 'If Devon learns I don't have the money in my possession, he'll have kittens.'

'You mean he'll become upset?'

'Exactly. Now we don't want Devon to worry. That means that if I talk to him, I'll have to lie about having the money. I don't want to lie, either . . . but think of it as a temporary condition on behalf of a good cause.'

'The widows and orphans?'

'No. My hide.'

'Oh. Yo comprendo.'

'Grand.' And the only thing your brilliant plan doesn't take into account, he thought, is that maybe Angie is headed for Mexico . . . or *Europe*, for that matter, with the Foundation's cash.

They investigated the first place, a courtyard cluster of cabins called the E-Z Rest Motel, as discreetly as possible. No Firebird, no Mustang.

'Strike one,' Michael said, backing out of the E-Z's driveway.

'*I may have something, Michael,*' KITT said after a few more miles.

'Let's have it.'

'*I've just registered radio requests for motor vehicle identification via the sheriff's department's patch-in to the state-wide computer records. The most recent one is for us – I must say their description of me as a "sports car" isn't very flattering.*'

Michael nodded. They checked him out as soon as he passed the 'Welcome to Gatesville' sign. Maybe they had done the same for Angie and Roberto. 'Trace it back as far as you can KITT.'

'*Michael, what's a "vanity plate?*"'

He grinned at the innocent way the question was posed. 'That's your licence plate, KITT. Since it reads K-N-I-G-H-T, that's what they call it.'

'*I don't think I like that, either.*'

'I copy,' he said. 'Anything on the police computer?'

'*No. But Devon is still calling.*'

'Tell him *no en casa.*'

'*You might as well face up to it, Michael.*'

He had a sudden idea that might cut around all this smoke – if he could find out where KITT's cabin mike was, he could turn on his portable electric razor and perch it right next to the pickup, shouting over it. Devon would read it as interference, and thus know Michael was still alive and kicking and above all, *willing* to communicate, but 'unable' to do so, thanks to some atmospheric disturbance.

'Say, KITT. Offhand, do you know where your interior cabin mike is?'

'*Certainly, Michael. I have comprehensive data on all facets of my layout. The pickups through which you and I talk while you're in the car, plus the radio patch, are located inside the padded roll bar next to your head for maximum sensitivity.*'

A visual blinked onto one of the monitors, fixing the location of the microphones.

'Great,' said Michael, switching on the AUTO CRUISE mode and grabbing for his toilet kit. 'Tell Devon I'll be on in a second.'

'He'll be relieved, Michael, what are you doing?'

'Never mind. A surprise.'

'Michael, I've completed my trace. At four-thirty this afternoon sheriff's car B-4, local, requested motor vehicle ID on a green Pontiac Firebird, licence number 375 RKJ, southeastbound on the same road we're on right now.'

'Bingo!' Michael touched the vox-box with his finger, the equivalent to a pat on the back for KITT. 'You're a first-class sleuth. That means we're on the right trail after all – now all we have to do is catch up.'

It also meant bad news for Roberto. Michael thought. Angie was using his car, and he doubted now whether they were together. She would have found it difficult to make such good travel time with a critically wounded man in tow. They would have had to stop somewhere along the line . . . if he was still alive, and not lying dead in a culvert somewhere between here and Houston.

The next place was called – charmingly – the Rodeo Sleep-Stop.

The only car parked in front of a bungalow was a lime-green Firebird.

It was 9:30 p.m.; dark had settled in for the night.

Angie picked her way along the black-country road in Roberto's Firebird. She had decided at the last minute not to involve her sister Monica; that would be the first place the Stones would look for her, anyway. Needing time to think out what her next move would be, and time to rest from running, she had checked into the rundown little motel by the side of the road . . . leaving Monica blissfully ignorant and safely uninvolved.

After sunset she had decided to leave the room – the dark, too, was comfortingly safe – and rustle up some dinner. There was a take-out chicken place near a local high school, and not far from that in Gatesville she had found a convenience market, where she picked up a few toiletries and other items she had not packed in her mad rush to get clear of the apartment on Big Rock Road.

Her hair was twisted and frayed. She needed sleep after

111

the harried events that had begun with her early morning visit to Roberto Laguna's room at Mercy General. She was relieved to see that nothing had changed in the Rodeo Sleep-Stop's courtyard since she left, except for the presence of a battered Ford pickup truck in the lot directly across from her bungalow. Someone else had checked in in the hour or so she had been shopping, and the room lights were already out. Teenagers, she guessed, having a night on the town.

The lights in the small motel office were down, too, and somebody was watching TV in a back room. The hypnotic blue glow lit up the windows.

She parked, grabbed her bags, and dug for her key on its faded wooden paddle. Cabin Four. The light by the windows was still on, as she'd left it.

'Buenos noches.'

At the sight of Michael Knight sitting easily in the chair across from the door, Angie's bags dropped, scattering their contents across the floor of the room. Her arms froze, as though they were still holding the bags.

The American 180 lay, just as easily, across Michael's lap.

From the bed, Roberto Laguna said, 'Come on in, Angie. Close the door.' Roberto's hair hung lankly and there were dark circles beneath his eyes. He had obviously been through an ordeal. Sweat stained his clothing, and the dressings on his arm, inside a dirty sling, begged to be changed. There was a single crutch leaning close to the bed, for his leg wound.

'Come on in, Angie,' said Michael. 'So nice to see you again. I want you to put your purse on the floor by the strap and kick it across to me. Don't kick it too hard; we wouldn't want your gun to go off, right? Might hurt somebody.'

She did as she was told, the fight draining out of her. The day had exhausted her and she had nothing left.

Michael stopped the bag with his foot, leaned over and checked it. Inside he found a five-shot .32-calibre revolver. He took it and jacked the rounds out onto the floor, where they rolled in different directions. None had been fired.

'How did you find us?' she said, closing the door. 'I can't

112

believe you found us. . . .'

'A little science, a little luck, a little logic, and a hell of a lot of anger,' said Michael. 'I'd prefer not to hoist up this monster gun here and point it at you, so why don't we just talk? I'll ask questions and you give me answers, how's that?' Michael figured he was entitled to this sadistic little scene.

Angie ignored the junk on the floor and walked across to Roberto. He embraced her with his good arm; they kissed. 'Let's do what he says, babe,' Roberto said softly. 'I can't run, not this way. I thought I could but I can't.'

Ignoring Michael for a second Angie said, 'I've brought dressings, antiseptic, other things. I'll fix you up.'

'Roberto and I have been having a civil little discussion,' said Michael. The smell of the spilled fried chicken was making him hungry. 'About how you used to be a nurse, among other things. It seems I keep getting in trouble by underestimating you.'

Angie collected the medical supplies from the floor. 'I'm going to need some hot water to wash all this junk off with,' he said, indicating Roberto's tattering dressing and dirty arm.

Michael had already checked out the bathroom. It was clean of potential weapons and its window was too small to permit escape. 'Go ahead,' he said. 'But keep in sight.'

As Angie worked, continually brushing hair out of her face, Roberto said to her, 'He got in while I was stumping around in the bathroom. I didn't hear a sound. And there wasn't too much I could do, at any rate. So here we are.' He let his other arm drop limply on the bed. He was near total exhaustion himself.

'When I'd heard you visited Roberto's room at Mercy General after Father Carlos left,' said Michael, 'I figured you'd added assassination to your long list of accomplishments. You stole his car and took it on the lam, I figured. What I *didn't* figure was that I'd find you and Roberto together . . . and not shooting at each other.'

Angie re-emerged with a tray of hot, soapy water and some hotel-issue towels and washcloths. She arranged them

113

on the bed and began to professionally strip the bandages and clean Roberto's injuries.

'How much of the money is already gone, Angie?' Michael had found and checked the briefcase already, but was curious as to what her reply might be.

'Four hundred dollars and some change short,' she said without looking at him. 'Helicopters aren't cheap to rent, you know.'

'So it wasn't the Stones that flew you away from Crombie's abandoned gas station?'

'Hey, man,' said Roberto. 'You caught us; you got your money back. What do you want from us?'

'Why, Roberto, old buddy, I want my damned four hundred bucks back. And I want the truth from this lady here, for a change of pace. Talk, Angie, and talk fast – why the hell did you have to set me up?' Michael's hands automatically cradled the machine gun.

'I wanted to buy some time,' she said, sighing. 'If you thought the Stones had robbed you, and the Stones thought you'd lit out on them, you'd be after each other so much that neither of you would bother looking for me . . . and Roberto and I could get away.' She wrung out a cloth over the bowl. Grey water and dry blood came away.

'Roberto . . . and you?'

'We've been lovers for nearly a year now. The Stones don't know.'

'Neither do the Lagunas,' said Roberto.

'But you couldn't keep it to yourself,' said Michael, piecing events together in reverse. 'So you told your brother about Angie in confession.'

Roberto nodded gravely.

'We realized we *couldn't* be in love, not in Houston, not with the Lagunas at war with the Stones. We wanted to leave, to start fresh someplace else . . . but we didn't have the kind of money that takes.'

'Until I came along with my handy briefcase,' Michael said, feeling like a first-class dupe. 'And Father Carlos doesn't bother to tell you about me, because then you'd know he gave away your girlfriend's name. He just didn't want to finger *you*.' And after all that bilge about the sanctity of the confessional! Michael was rapidly getting sick of the whole Laguna family.

'Don't you get it, Michael? Are you so dumb you can't see we had no choice?' said Angie.

'I see it too well,' he said. 'Romeo and Juliet all over again. But somehow I'm not touched.'

Roberto's eyes flared. 'Who are you to talk, eh? To judge? You would sell weapons to the Stones, or to anybody who would give you money!'

Michael shook his head. 'You poor dupe. I don't deal in illegal weapons; I *say* I deal in illegal weapons. There's a difference.'

Angie stopped working, aghast. 'Then just who are you? What do you want?'

Michael considered a longwinded explanation, then said, 'It doesn't really matter. I was recruited by Father Carlos to help stop the warfare between the Lagunas and the Stones. I want the Stones out of business – for my own reasons. Father Carlos gave me Angie's name as a Stones contact – but didn't tell Roberto, for obvious reasons. Obvious now. He knew you were in love; he did not approve, but he still wants the Stones out of everyone's hair.'

Roberto shook his head. '*Mi hermano, Madré de Dios*, what a mess.'

'Angie, what were the Stones doing the whole time you were leading me on that fun-ride through the desert earlier today?'

'Waiting for you up at Tower Rock Pass with a truckload of arms. They're gonna be angry.'

'I can lie about needing more time to get the money,' he said. 'I've still got to stop that shipment, and the best way to stop it is to buy it.' He dug through Angie's purse and came up with a wallet full of credit cards.

'Hey! What are you doing!'

'You, my bright young lady, are going down to the friendly Gatesville general store, or whatever they call it around here, and use these to even out my two hundred and forty grand. I've got a buy to make tomorrow. Then you're

115

coming back to Houston with me.'

'I'm – ? You mean you'd trust me?' Her tone indicated that if their positions were reversed, she would not trust him.

'I need you as an alibi for being late. I saw the way Ricky was pawing at you; he'll believe what you tell him.'

At the mention of Ricky's name, Roberto unleashed a string of curses in Spanish.

'And what do you want me to tell Ricky?' she said, eying Michael doubtfully.

'That you and I were together tonight. That takes care of both my problem *and* yours.'

Roberto clearly did not approve, but reconsidered and saw the plan to be the lesser of two evils. He was obviously very much in love with Angie, though Michael doubted that he could handle a personality like hers for very long himself. She was too much like a werewolf, like Liberty Cox – always changing into something else, unexpectedly.

'I can't,' she said. 'This is our chance to get out, and if we don't get out now . . .'

'Angie, there's more at stake here than just you and Roberto. The massacre of Roberto's family will continue until there isn't a Laguna left in Texas. You know how the Stones operate. And if my plan works, you two will have the new beginning you keep jabbering about. *Think*, woman! You have to walk away from this clean, not sneak away in the middle of the night!'

Roberto watched Michael dourly. 'You should be a priest.'

'Angie, I need your help to pull this thing off. I won't say you owe it to me. I don't care. Just look at it for yourself and you'll see what I'm talking about.'

She hesitated, torn and undecided. There was really no choice. With Michael and the money gone, they were back where they started . . . only with Roberto wounded, and the war very much alive.

'Roberto . . .' she began.

'Shh,' he said, wrapping his left arm around her and pulling her close. 'Go with him. Go ahead. Then come back to me. If we can eliminate the Stones, we'll approach my brother again. If everything is as this man says, it will be so. Angie – he's saved my life once already, by getting me to the hospital after the raid on my sister's wedding party. I have a debt to him. You can pay it. And we can all walk away clean, as he says.'

While Michael collected the rest of the stuff on the floor – incuding a drumstick, which he bit into ravenously – Angie said, 'I'll be back as soon as I can.'

They kissed, and five minutes later Roberto was alone again in the motel room.

The sound of the car pulling out had long faded. Roberto sat dispiritedly on the bed munching the remains of the cold fried chicken. His stomach was full but he was uneasy.

Seen in his new role as some kind of nonspecific, outside diplomat, Michael Knight seemed even more of an enigma. The Laguna clan was not accustomed to outsiders blithely popping in, with such good timing, offering to solve all their problems for them, fight their battles for them . . . do everything for them . . .

Roberto suspected that he would eventually pick up the phone by the bed, and charge a call to his room number. When he did, a line buzzed softly and then was picked up somewhere in Houston.

'*Bueno.*'

'*Eduardo – es Roberto,*' he said. 'Don't talk, just listen. I know how we can find the *Corazones de Piedras.*'

11

Michael could have sworn he heard Devon make a strangling noise on the other end of the radiophone line.

'Look, Devon, it's okay *now* –' Michael said, weary but a bit amused.

'Michael,' came Devon's voice, 'don't tell me that you lost the money.' His tone suggested that Michael's own death might not be as catastrophic.

'I didn't lose the money.'

'Then why have you been avoiding me, dodging my calls to KITT?'

Now came the creative part. 'Well, I didn't lose the money, Devon . . . but I did run into a few problems along the way.'

Devon's voice came back with dead certainty. 'You lost the money.'

'I *misplaced* the money . . .'

The strangled noise came over the line again.

'. . . but I got it back, too.'

'I sensed something had happened of which I might not approve,' Devon admonished. 'Michael, the Foundation's

Charity Benefit Fund is for –'

'Widows and orphans, I know,' said Michael. 'I got the scoop from KITT. You worry too bloody much, Devon old man. Hang on a minute.'

KITT was parked near an Exxon station in downtown Houston. About ten yards away, Angie was shut up in a phone booth, presumably calling the Stones and setting up Michael's alibi. Michael saw her finish and hang up. There was that split instant of hesitation before leaving the booth that all human beings share – [the wait for the sound of the money dropping into Ma Bell's pocket.] Then she returned to the car.

'Well? How'd it go down?'

She fidgeted with her hands in her lap. 'D.D. bought it. I'm not so sure about Ricky, but I think that just might be jealousy and not suspicion. He'd like to "claim" me, or some dumb caveman thing like that, and probably resents the idea I'd find someone more dashing than his sweaty iron-pumping, rough-talking *macho* trip. But I also think that, in this case, business will overrule pleasure. Two hundred and forty grand isn't a small buy-in.'

'Any conditions?' said Michael. Devon's incoming call was blinking on hold.

'Yeah. They want to see the money before anything else happens, because you didn't show up yesterday. They're in a room at the Shanghai Inn, downtown.'

'We're supposed to meet them there?'

'A.S.A.P., as soon as possible. They want us both to show up.'

'We'd better get that part over with, then. Will the buy still go down today?'

'If they're pleased with the cash. I don't see why not.' Mention of the money stung Angie. Michael had stood over her earlier while she walked into a Houston bank and pumped her meagre savings account dry to replace the cash she had used for the helicopter. He watched while she laboriously read off the serial numbers of the bills for KITT to record via the voice-monitor. If there was any trouble, KITT could then cross-reference the numbers with

120

Devon's to coordinate a search for them. It seemed a bit cruel . . . but Michael was not about to put up the missing cash himself. Let Angie pay a bit to learn a lesson, he thought.

Michael punched a glowing crystal button on the function panel to the right of the steering column. It beeped with a touch-tone sound.

'Devon?'

'Still here, Michael.'

'We're going to check in with the Stones right now. I'll call you as soon as I've got news. Give my love to Bonnie, y'hear?'

There was a characteristic Devon pause, then: 'If I tell her that, she'll ask me if you're feeling all right, or are ill.'

'I know,' said Michael, and then, to Angie, 'Well . . . let's do it.'

The Shanghai Inn was a cluster of modernistic two-storey hotel buildings jazzed up with some fake Oriental trappings and a lot of heavy brown lumber – as beams, as timbers, as ambience. Michael parked in the lot and let Angie lead him to the room the Stones were waiting in. Once again, he was not packing a gun . . . for luck. The American 180 was locked in KITT's trunk, safety on. KITT's scanners ran full blast while Michael was away from the car.

They stopped at a second-storey door, anonymously numbered like so many urban hotels, totally devoid of identity. She gave him a queasy glance, still looking for reassurance, then rapped on the door.

No secret code-knock, Michael thought.

D.D.'s moustachioed face peered out over the security chain. The door slammed, then re-opened.

'Glad you could finally make it, ace,' he said, with a trace of sarcasm.

They entered a two-room suite. Beer cans and cigarette butts adorned the window table. The colour TV was on but the sound was dead. A woman with a blazing green-and-orange face laughed like a donkey as she won some throwaway prize on a game show.

121

Ricky stood by the twin bed, hands locked behind his back, impassive. He had on a web-mesh muscle-builder tank top and a brown leather vest that was a bit damp at the armpits.

'I had a vision there would be trouble,' he intoned. 'Are you bringing me more trouble . . . boy?'

Michael gestured with the briefcase. 'Not unless you count this as bad news,' he said, inwardly delighting at his little personal irony. If the Stones accepted the money, they could be traced and there *would* be trouble. He cleared some of the junk from a dresser top – without being asked; to wait for these goons to direct him would mean trouble as well – and laid the briefcase down, his hands pausing on the silver clasps.

'Well?' he said.

Ricky worked a bit of food lodged in his teeth, using his tongue, speaking slowly and lugubriously. 'What happened to you yesterday . . . boy?'

'Hit a few delays,' said Michael.

Ricky turned on Angie, who nearly cringed. 'I'll just bet you did.' For a moment, Michael did not exist in the room. 'How come you trot off with this cowboy on a moment's notice?' beefed Ricky. 'What about you and me?' He clamped his fingers around Angie's forearm now.

Behind Ricky's back D.D. gave Michael an exaggerated shrug, mouthing the word *amor*. Who could tell, eh, what makes people in love so crazy?

Angie found some of her old crust. 'Let got of my arm!' She whipped it free, the gesture of defiance clearly not in Ricky's plan.

He fumed for a moment. 'What's that guy got I ain't got?'

She moved across the room toward D.D and tried to find something to drink. 'For one thing,' she returned, 'a clean shirt.'

D.D. laughed.

'For another thing,' Michael cut in, 'this.' He again indicated the briefcase. 'Do you want to see this, or do you want to play games, big mercenary?'

Ricky shot a parting look at Angie. 'I'll deal with you

later,' he muttered, cursing. He pointed from D.D. to the briefcase. 'Count it.'

Michael snapped open the case. The cash was all there, in military little rows.

D.D. thumbed through the stacks, licking his finger as he went.

'Aren't you going to pat me down this afternoon?' Michael said cheerfully.

Ricky either did not notice, or was still busy glaring meaningfully – he thought – at Angie. Perhaps using the fiction that he and Angie were out cavorting somewhere as an excuse for being late was the wrong approach, considering Ricky's somewhat limited concept of *machismo*. If only he knew, thought Michael, that his real competition had the last name of Laguna.

Keeping up his tough-for-tough facade, Michael said, 'Got anything cold to drink around this dump? It's a steambath in here. Smells like a locker room.'

'Check out the cooler,' said D.D., not looking up from the case.

Ricky went to the closet and pulled down an oblong suitcase, lifting it gingerly down onto one of the beds and unlatching it. Nestled in a bed of air-bag plastic bubbles inside was a shining new copy of the American 180 – without a clip. Wordlessly he handed it across to Michael.

The gun was by now familiar in Michael's hands. He hefted it and mock-sighted. He looked for the Lexington serial number, and chambered the bolt once to make sure the system was bona fide and not an exterior copy – as a professional would have done.

'A pretty piece,' he said. 'Got me out of a lot of jams in the past.' He handed the weapon back to Ricky. 'What about the Nunn Nineteens?'

'Tomorrow.' Ricky said. 'You expecting any *problems* at the crack of dawn?' He was looking at Angie while he said it, and Michael could almost read his thoughts. The blond man hated the idea that Angie did not find him attractive and physically irresistible.

'It's all present and accounted for,' announced D.D.,

closing the briefcase.

'Okay,' said Ricky. 'Tomorrow morning, oh-seven-hundred hours at Tower Rock Pass – where the peaks are the highest.'

'He's got this thing about being close to the eagles,' said D.D. as if it explained anything. 'His Injun spirit-brothers.'

Ricky ignored his partner.

'You be there with the guns; I'll be there with the money. Relax, Ricky.' Michael picked up the briefcase again.

'I don't give people second chances,' said Ricky. 'It's bad for the *mana*, the spiritual force. *Mana* is wasted by delays, by nonproductivity. You have wasted our *mana* with your . . . dalliance.' Now he sounded absurdly pious. 'I warn you,' he said, his voice low and precise again, 'be there tomorrow morning. Or it will not be a matter of finding yourself another seller. It will be a matter of living to find one, and of begging to live. Do you understand?'

'I'll be there,' said Michael.

There was another knock on the door.

Ricky faded back against the wall, breaking loose his ugly Schmeisser machine pistol from its shoulder holster. He waved D.D. to the door. The snout of the weapon was centred on Michael.

'Any provocative action,' Ricky hissed, 'and you are the first to die. I can kill you both in two seconds flat.' He motioned for Michael and Angie to back away, over by the beds.

'It's Alemán,' said D.D., his eyeball glued to the door peephole.

Ricky nodded, holstering his piece.

D.D. opened the door to admit a slightly built man dressed in a Continental suit. He was short but compact in build, finely attired down to the polished Gucci shoes on his tiny dancer's feet. He looked rather like an Italian movie star.

He bowed formally to Ricky. 'We have an appointment, yes?'

Ricky relaxed. 'Mister Alemán,' he said, by way of introduction. 'Some other friends of ours were just leaving.'

D.D. lingered by the door.

'I guess we were,' said Michael. 'Come on, Angie, let's go.'

He took several steps toward the door when Ricky casually interrupted. 'Mr . . . ah, Knight here knows a friend of yours, Mr Alemán.'

'Indeed?' said Alemán with polite but passing interest. His eyebrows were up, his expression waiting for Michael to clarify.

'Yeah,' said Ricky. 'Emile Pavlon.'

Michael felt a nervous lump crystalize in his throat. Maybe this was some kind of bizarre test.

Alemán's expression was bland, but apparently friendly and utterly open. 'You know Emile?'

Michael licked his lips against the heat blasting in through the door and nodded. 'Right . . . Emile and I met in South America. Belize.'

The visitor nodded, as if understanding what that meant. 'Emile was one of my closest friends, but regrettably I've not seen him of late. I have an aversion to Guatemala, you see, and an even bigger aversion to prison.'

Ricky and D.D. laughed.

Michael smiled uneasily. 'I know what you mean.'

'It is always nice to meet an ally of Emile's, even if it is an ex-ally for the time being,' said Alemán. 'And if you should encounter Emile before I do, tell him that Giorgio Alemán sends his regards. Yes?'

'Sure,' said Michael, shaking the man's proffered hand. 'We have to go, and you obviously have business to attend to.'

He and Angie stepped out, and D.D. closed the door.

Halfway down the open-air breezeway Michael said, 'Do you know that guy?'

'Never saw him before,' said Angie.

'I sure hope we're still in the clear,' he said. 'That was nearly too close for my taste.'

'Sounds like the deal's still on. Ricky could have said no, shut the whole thing down, and run to earth again.'

'Come on, let's get back to the car. I've got to call

Devon.'

'That won't do any good,' said Angie. 'They'll be gone from here in fifteen minutes, and they've only brought one gun with them.'

'No, you're thinking too far ahead. We need to catch them in possession of the whole shipment. Lacking that, we need to get them with the money tomorrow morning.'

Just offhand, the prospect of another day-long wait generated acid in Michael's stomach. Twenty-four hours, he thought. Twenty-four hours and the whole sequence would be done, and he could head back to California.

D.D. cracked himself a fresh beer, offering another can to Alemán, the visitor, who declined

'You know the guy?' Ricky said.

Alemán pursed his lips and shook his head sadly. 'He is a stranger to me. I have never seen him before. Do you suspect he is with the Lagunas?'

Ricky nodded. 'That's the most obvious choice. Those poor suckers have been trying to fix us for a whole year now, and they always show up to raid us twenty-four hours after we've vacated.'

'We're cookin' a little surprise for them tomorrow,' D.D. added.

The visitor nodded approvingly. 'So, gentleman. Was I on time.'

'Right on cue,' said Ricky. To D.D.: 'Pay the man.'

D.D. began to peel off large-denomination bills from a wad in his pocket.

'Nice of you to supply this bonus,' said the European, 'Considering everything else you've done for me.'

'No sweat,' said D.D. 'It's always a pleasure doing business with *you*, Emile.'

12

'Where to?' Michael said. He, KITT, and Angie were cruising the streets of Houston.

'How about the Embers?' she said. 'I have plenty of time to put in there. In case you forgot, we just emptied my savings account, and I'd like to get around to putting something back in.'

Michael let it pass. He felt tired, and running tomorrow morning's agenda through his head over and over would acomplish little beyond gaining him a walloping thumper of a headache. He made a gradual path toward the Houston Plaza. His thoughts about the fresh, clean bed waiting in his hotel room were tempting, and he actually found he had to keep himself from nodding off at the wheel.

Angie interpreted his silence as pique. 'You're not still angry with me . . . I hope?'

'Right now I'm more concerned with who that foreign fellow back there might've been.'

'Who do you think he was?' Angie was talking mostly to reassure herself that she wasn't alone. She'd been caught by Michael, and a punishment of sorts had been levied, and now she wanted more than anything for things to get back to normal. Or appear to balance out after all this trouble and anguish, all the blood and violence. . . .

'Can't tell,' said Michael. 'I suppose it *could* have just been a fluke. Another customer with an appointment to buy guns. Maybe my guns. But what were the Stones selling that guy if I was buying their whole stock of Nunn Nineteens and American 180s? What if he's the guy they're selling the Malko cartridge launchers to? That stuff will go straight to Central America . . . and that's one of the things I'm supposed to be here to stop.'

'Who hired you?' said Angie. 'Father Carlos? Roberto's brother?'

'Nobody hired me,' said Michael. 'I'm an independent contractor, as they say. I heard the Lagunas were in trouble, learned what I could, and decided to intercede. So – don't you want to go get your own car, so you can drive home from work?'

'No. I don't want to go back to that dinge-hole. I want to go back and see Roberto.'

'Why don't we let that wait till tomorrow morning?' he said pondering. 'KITT, did you scan anyone coming in after we entered the Shanghai Inn? Short, compact, European-looking?'

The modulator on KITT's vox-box jumped up and down in syllabic cadence with the car's reply: '*I monitored the entrances, Michael, and in the fifteen or so minutes you spent inside I recorded the traffic. A spot-review shows no person such as you just described, but I can run the tape again for you, if you wish.*'

'Do that,' said Michael.

Angie was goggling. 'What was *that*? A radio or something?' Now she was staring at the Super Dash uncertainly. 'Another one of those gadgets you're always talking about? The thing that locks the doors –?'

The explanation seemed to stretch to infinity before his mind's eye. Instead of launching into a recitation, he simply said. 'There's a . . . sort of a computer hooked into the car. Microprocessing units. Microchip –'

'That makes it talk? The car, I mean?'

'It's a voice-activated computer, that's all,' he said, although he knew KITT would have an argument for that one. 'Look, Angie, I'm going to have KITT run the tape. Watch it with me, will you, and let's see if we can spot that guy we met in Ricky's room?'

'KITT?' she said, still confused.

'That's my . . . er, good friend at the computer console,' he said.

'Mighty kind of you to say so,' KITT added, wryly.

'Run the tape,' he said, pulling into the parking lot of the Houston Plaza and killing the engine. He was growing to hate having to explain KITT's intricacies to every passenger who spent time in the seat opposite him. The explanation was usually lost; riders regarded the car initially with astonishment and came to accept its remarkable abilities quite trustingly. Michael, on the other hand, felt the more he learned about the technology that went into KITT, the more he could not believe such things were really possible – and he was 'closer' to KITT, he felt, than anyone. The car had become his indestructible, multitalented partner . . . after he had sworn he would never again use partners. By using KITT, he slowly discovered that he had retained the advantages of having a partner, a backup, without the liabilities of one – namely, the regrettable tendency of Michael's past backups to get shot up, knocked down, or blown apart.

He refocused his attention on the tape playback, which they sat watching in the parking lot. On both of KITT's screens, people moved in and out of the automatic doors to the Shanghai Inn . . . totally unaware that they were being monitored.

'Angie,' said Michael. 'You're *sure* you never saw that man before?'

It was the one question that could hurt her, and it showed. 'No. He's a stranger. Michael, I'm not asking you to excuse the fact that I lied to you before, but I'm not lying to you now. I'm done with that.'

'I'd really like to believe that,' Michael said encouragingly.

'You can.'

The tape spun out, revealing nothing, eating time. When it was done, they had seen no indication of the mysterious European supposedly named Giorgio Alemán.

'I don't understand,' said Angie. 'If he had an appointment . . .'

'He would have arrived right on time,' said Michael. 'The Stones seem real big on precise timing; it's very military. Yet this new guy shows up in the middle of *our* meeting, and without walking through the door. I suppose he could have been in the hotel already, in a room or something, but . . .' He shook his head. Nothing connected.

'If he was,' said Angie, 'then why bother with a meeting at all? They should be dropping in on him, not vice versa.'

'Unless it was some kind of setup.' He rubbed his chin. 'KITT – have we got any kind of visual on Emile Pavlon yet?' Previously, Michael had only got the man's name and biography, from the files.

'*No, Michael. I suggest you contact Devon.*'

'Yeah. I just hope our old buddy Roberto stays put for the time being.'

'He'll wait at the motel,' said Angie. 'Why wouldn't he stay there? He loves me and I think he trusts your plan . . . till tomorrow morning, at least.'

'He's been in love with you for a year, Angie . . . but he's been a Laguna for a lifetime, and that might work against my plan.'

'Will I see you after work?'

'Call my room. 2007.'

'Okay,' she said. 'I'd like that.'

As she walked off across the parking lot, Michael noticed that her stride seemed to have regained some of the jauntiness he remembered from the first time he'd seen her. She was 'legit' again.

'Alright, KITT, let's get Devon on the horn,' he said, punching the communications toggle.

'Michael, Devon isn't available.'

He stared dumbfounded at the speaker grille, then

laughed. The old fox had turned the tables on him again. Maybe he had even thought of the razor trick.

Michael locked up KITT and headed for his room in the Plaza.

Houston's skyline was mauve and pink with twilight. The heat of the day had not yet dissipated from the sidewalks and pavement, but the brilliant light, at least, was toning down for the night.

Michael thought he heard someone pounding on his room door. He ignored it until he heard it again, more clearly.

He cranked the needle spray of the shower to a full stop and listened, amidst the sound of dripping water and the vigorous slurping of the drain, to the knocking.

He was expecting no visitors until Angie got off at around two a.m. Perhaps there was trouble.

He wound a skimpy hotel towel round himself – when damp it was very nearly transparent anyway – and put his eye to the peephole, keeping to one side of the door just in case Ricky and D.D. were standing outside with changed minds and loaded automatics, ready to blow him away through the door itself.

Michael saw a grotesquely magnified and distorted version of Devon Miles's face, glancing up and down the corridor outside.

'Devon!' he said, opening the door to admit the older man.

Devon paused on the threshold to give Michael the once-over. Eyeing the towel, he said, 'On your way out for the night? To a toga party, perhaps?'

Michael deliberately crossed the room after the door was shut and exchanged the towel for his pants. He clicked on a table lamp. 'What's up? Why the personal appearance?'

Devon gave this some thought. 'If I said I was just "in the neighbourhood," you probably wouldn't believe me.'

'No more than you'd believe that I'm on my way to the circus to be the Human Cannonball.'

Devon gnawed at his lip and paid too much attention to the straightening of his trouser creases.

131

'What is it, already?'

'I want you to cancel the weapons buy tomorrow.'

'*What?!*' Michael was unsure he'd heard clearly. 'No can do, *señor*. You know what I had to go through this afternoon to convince those goons that my disappearing act yesterday was legitimate? They were ready to blow me away in the hotel room. In fact, one of them held a gun this far from my nose just this afternoon.' He held an imaginary pistol a foot from Devon's face.

'Listen, Michael. I've been in almost constant touch with the authorities in Guatemala. Emile Pavlon escaped from Torreon Prison the day before yesterday.'

Silence hung between them and Michael sat heavily down on the bed.

'Boy, oh boy. Thanks for letting me know. I really appreciate that, Devon, old chap – *now* what the hell do we do? I'm almost sure I met Pavlon this afternoon, and blew my own cover to the Stones. He was going under the name Giorgio Alemán. I'm sure *that* wasn't in KITT's dossier.'

'Any doubt?' said Devon, trying to consider all possible courses of action.

'Plenty. If it wasn't Pavlon, I'm still clear for the buy tomorrow. Why panic and cancel?'

'Because Pavlon had help! Someone bribed the guards and conducted him out of the country – that takes *baksheesh* – something the Stones can certainly muster if they really needed it.'

'It could have been someone else,' said Michael. 'One of Pavlon's own friends. Have you come up with a wirephoto of him, or anything yet?'

'No visual ID. *That* was one of Pavlon's specialties – deep cover.' Devon folded his hands in his lap. The situation was clearly ominous to him.

'Pavlon certainly had contacts, employees, other people who would want to bribe him out of jail.' When Devon offered no response, Michael pressed: '*Right?*'

'Michael, it could have been the Stones just as easily. Pavlon had been in Torreon for nearly two years. Doesn't it strike you as curious that he escaped the day after you used his name to boost up your cover?'

Michael resented being asked to walk away after all this time and hassle and risk.

'I appreciate your commitment to a mission you had no desire to undertake in the first place,' said Devon. 'I'm thankful for your decision, and I admire your courage. I do not, however, wish to mourn your death . . . and if the Stones have proven to themselves that you are not the person you represent yourself to be, they shall surely kill you at oh-seven-hundred hours. And we all lose.'

'What about the people who lose if we sit here and do nothing?' returned Michael. 'The people who will die simply because they know someone named Laguna, or have the misfortune to have been born with the name themselves? The people in South America . . .?'

Quietly, Devon conceded. 'As always, Michael, the decision rests with you.' He rose and started for the room door. 'If you decide not to take the chance tomorrow morning, let me know. Call me.'

'And if I don't call?' He stood there, barechested, wearing only his pants. The damp towel covered one of his bare feet.

'I'll be waiting on standby, of course.'

'Wait a second, Devon, I'm thinking.' He put his fingers to his lips and paced around the room. 'Can you talk Bonnie into getting the truck here, or marrying up with me on the highway somewhere – as fast as possible?'

'I'm sure it can be arranged.' He moved immediately for the hotel room telephone.

'Good.'

'What's your plan?' Devon said, his finger pausing above the touchtone keyboard.

'Something Bonnie mentioned earlier about putting special ordnance into KITT for each mission,' said Michael. 'I just thought of a little extra that might save all of us.'

Michael's habitual method of slotting KITT into the rearward bay of the Knight Industries service rig was to pace it at fifty miles per hour, then accelerate up the retractable ramp as both truck and car continued to move along the highway. Several hours following Devon's room visit, the two men were eastbound out of Houston, heading for a rendezvous point in the middle of the desert with Bonnie Barstow and the truck.

When the rear gate of the truck loomed large in the front windshield, and KITT gave the sensor peep that indicated both the car and the truck were paced for synchronous entry, Devon turned to Michael with a waxy complexion and asked why they couldn't just stop and plug the car into the back of the truck 'manually,' as he put it.

'Don't worry. Devon, this is as safe as falling asleep. I've done this a hundred times by now.'

'Yes, but *I've* never done it.'

'First time for everything. Hang on!'

With a bump and a rush of acceleration, they moved up into the truck bed. Devon's fingers were white on the armrests.

'See? Not so bad.'

'My impetuous youth is far behind me,' he muttered. 'Too far.'

'And here's the good doctor Barstow to welcome us at this late hour,' said Michael, getting out of the car. 'Hi, Bonnie.'

'This had better be a matter of life and death, as you're so fond of telling everyone,' Bonnie said. She looked as though she had just been rudely awakened; dark smudges from too little sleep had crept below her eyes.

'What's the matter, am I making somebody miss the late show on TV?'

'Oh, you . . .' She let it hang.

'Who's driving the truck?'

'Gates Cashman,' said Bonnie. 'One of the Knight techs.'

'Do I detect more than a note of passing interest in your voice for this young whiz kid?'

'No, you do not.'

Michael and Bonnie regularly enjoyed this sort of sparring: his offence and her defence. It substituted for any more substantial nonwork relationship between them, and despite the comic pains each of them took to avoid giving

134

ground, they had grown to like each other quite a bit – in secret, of course. Devon was not blind to this, nor did he ever feel the need to meddle. Something more pressing always, inevitably, demanded his time and energies. This did not stop him from wondering, in idle moments, if anything would grow out of the relationship between these two youngsters. Michael was dashing and intelligent; Bonnie was roundly capable and undeniably attractive. They were not polar opposites; on the contrary, they seemed to Devon to be so much alike in essence that their friendly bickering seemed the only safe way of coping. Devon provided a surrogate father image to complete the strange triangle, which centred around KITT and the Foundation's operational programme.

At least he'd not been trapped with boring people, he thought, thankful for tiny favours. He got out of the car and joined the pair in the small office/lounge section of the trailer.

'Bonnie, do KITT's smoke cylinders have to be modified if they were to hold . . . er, other substances?'

Once a problem was presented to her analytical mind, the ravishing Bonnie became all business. 'What sort of substance? They should hold anything except a high-grade corrosive.'

'I was thinking of tear gas, Mace, something like that,' said Michael.

'There's a possibility Michael's cover has been blown, as they say in the gangster movies,' said Devon. 'He's determined to meet the Stones tomorrow and consummate the weapons deal . . . even though they may be maintaining the buy as a setup just to kill him.'

'What I'm looking for is a highly concentrated, wide-dispersal gas that'll incapacitate everyone without harming them, to be sprayed from KITT's tanks like the smokescreen was. I need it to be quite dense and potent; we may have to take out guys on a hilltop above us by mere virtue of an updraft.'

Bonnie digested this. 'How about MR-90?'

'What is it?'

Devon cut in. 'A gas developed by the Army for field use against attacking infantry. They designed cannisters to be dropped by plane. It was like thick green fog; had virtually the same effects as tear gas . . . but it was too concentrated; it took out enemy and ally alike. It's absorbed through the pores, not by breathing; so protecting against it is quite laborious.'

'What if the Stones thought to bring gas masks to our little luau?'

'Wouldn't make any difference, unless they were inside body suits, totally sealed off. All you need is a square inch of explosed flesh.'

'I could make a terrible pun,' said Michael, 'but I won't.'

Bonnie narrowed her eyes at him, as if to say, *that's really awful!*

Devon cleared his throat to attract their attention. 'We're all a bit tired. Why don't we wrap this up. By tomorrow this time, we'll be headed back to home base.'

'A cheerful idea,' said Michael. 'Provided I'm still alive.'

'I rather like the plan,' said Bonnie. 'Fighting the Stones with their own kind of exclusive, sophisticated weaponry – only *this* time you'll be using something that they haven't got around to stealing yet.'

'Devon? Did Knight Industries help develop this gas Bonnie is talking about, too?'

'No, we had nothing to do with this particular piece of warmaking equipment. Besides, even the government ditched it – I'm afraid it was too pacifistic for their tastes, in addition to the drawback I've mentioned.'

'But it shouldn't affect you,' said Bonnie. 'Not if you're inside KITT, and remember to roll the windows up before you disperse it.' She waited a moment, then added a sly, wan smile. 'You *can* remember to keep the windows up, can't you?'

'For you, darling, I'll keep the windows up,' Michael said, expansively.

Bonnie snorted in laughter. 'Don't bother me, boys . . . I'm working. It'll take about an hour to switch over. There are snacks in the fridge.'

136

'You have this MR-90 on hand?' said Michael in surprise.

'I wouldn't mention it if I couldn't deliver it,' she said, moving to the storage cabinets below the workbench area.

'Thank goodness for anticipated contingencies,' mused Devon. He was clearly about to nod off right there in the chair.

Bonnie set to work, making a few other adjustments on and inside KITT before she was done. Michael helped her affix the drainage hoses to KITT's smoke emitter tanks, and for a brief time the dead desert surrounding the truck looked as though it had been teleported into the middle of a London pea-soup fogbank.

'I think that's got it,' she announced later, grease smudges on her forehead from crawling under the car. 'One thing, though. When you hit the button it'll evacuate the entire tank, so make sure you're in the right spot when you cut it loose.'

'You mean I only have one shot?'

'Yep,' she said. She gestured with a wrench. 'And I guarantee it'll go everywhere.' She racked the rest of her gear in the appropriate compartments. 'Gentlemen, I am going to shower and sleep. Good hunting, as the old flying aces used to say.'

'Why should we leave when you're just getting to the good part?' joked Michael.

'Get out of here before I brain you,' she said. 'And take care of my car.'

After dropping Devon off, Michael returned to the Plaza, thinking about resuming his shower. Trying to get some sleep was a fruitless idea; it was nearly dawn already.

When Michael opened his door – exercising the usual caution, bordering on paranoia, that his police experience had instilled in him – he found his room occupied. But not by a foe.

Angie was sprawled across the bed, still dressed for the most part in her Embers uniform, cuddling one pillow while her head rested on another. She was sound asleep, her shoes discarded on the floor.

137

There was a note on the desk on hotel stationery. It read:

Michael,
Hope you don't mind a sleep-in guest. I didn't want to leave and come back – waste of time.
    I left a message for a wake-up call at six o'clock, just in case.

A.

He put down the note, forcing himself to be preternaturally quiet, and crept back into the bathroom to finish his shower. When he came out, he found that she had not changed her position on the bed by an inch – she was that exhausted.

Michael got completely redressed for the sole purpose of going down to the lobby to make a phone call, instead of using the room phone. The elevator, the hallways, the lobby of the Plaza were mostly deserted. A couple of early-shift waitresses were brewing coffee in the downstairs restaurant.

Michael went to a hotel phone and billed his call to his room number. The call was placed through to Gatesville, to the Rodeo Sleep-Stop.

Roberto Laguna did not answer the phone.

You could not disconnect hotel phones – too many would be stolen that way – so they lacked the interchangeable component wires of normal house telephones. Roberto could not have disconnected his phone by tweezing the little catch and pulling out the wire. Nor was there a busy signal, to indicate the phone off the hook. The other end rang and rang, getting no response.

Of course, the Rodeo was a small operation. The room phones were probably patched through a switchboard in the office . . . which, as in most mom-and-pop motels, was shut down after ten p.m. No calls till morning.

Michael hung up. Give it another hour, he thought.

Then he returned to his room, and, watching Angie sleep, fell asleep himself, fully dressed, sitting in a chair.

13

'Roberto's gone.'

Michael's eyes slid open and for a moment he had to puzzle out reality to orient himself. Hotel room . . . still dark . . . Angie's legs.

His leg had cracked to the left while he slept, awkwardly, in the chair. Slowly, his body came to life, joints creaking. A pungent, pleasant smell wafted through the air and hit him agreeably in the nose.

Angie's legs were right in front of him, and his eyes slowly made the climb to her face.

'I called Gatesville,' she was saying. 'The motel room. No answer after twenty rings. So I called the main motel number for the Rodeo and got Mr Andersen, the old guy who checked me in. He says Roberto's car left several hours ago.'

Michael yawned and straightened. His clothing felt a bit stale. 'Did the car leave with Roberto in it?' he said around another jaw-cracking yawn.

'Mr Andersen says there's nobody in our room – no bags, nothing.'

Michael saw her now, clearly distraught, having been forced to put two and two together so soon after waking up. She stood there in her waitress get-up, wearing satiny nylons and no shoes, telling him all this while he was semiconscious.

Put it together, Michael, KITT might have told him. *You always do.*

'Is that coffee?' he said, nose pricking up.

Angie nodded. 'Room service. It's six-fifteen. God, I've put down three cups already. That's okay . . . I always order coffee for six when I'm staying at a hotel.'

Distract her with routine till you can focus your eyes, he thought. She needed to talk, to keep the anguish from backing up inside her – to talk about anything, just banal conversation, weather chat, anything. She was pouring him a cup of coffee, this woman he hardly knew, and the idea of coffee awoke his slowly stirring metabolism. He must have really been tired, he thought.

'How do you take it?'

He smiled. The smile was pretty good; it usually helped him get what he wanted. 'If you promise not to tell anybody, I take it black with sugar. That way, people think I'm drinking he-man coffee. Putting in cream would give away the deception.'

That eased her a bit. He saw her relax, visibly. He would re-introduce the topic of the missing Roberto when it was more strategic. When she brought the cup over (whisking it, nearly full to the brim, through the air with admirable balance), he took her hand and directed her to sit in the chair opposite him. Then he calmed her by rambling on for a minute. They had time yet.

'When I was four, my mom died. Bad scene all around. I took to getting up in the mornings to see my day before he rushed off to work. He was a heavy cigarette smoker and a big-league coffee drinker. I wanted to be like my dad, so he would get up in the morning and fix two cups of coffee. He loaded mine with about five pounds of sugar and a gallon of milk, then would hand it to me just as I came bopping down the stairs – in pajamas with feet, clutching a stuffed animal –

140

expecting my coffee like a real adult. It's the only really fundamental memory I have of my father.' He shrugged, looking just embarrassed enough to rouse Angie's sympathy and get her mind off their immediate problems. 'I weaned myself off the milk and sugar over the years . . . but every cup I drink has a direct lifeline to those first ones. I think of my old man whenever I sit down to coffee. It's my way of remembering him.'

Something clicked in Michael's mind – something not pressingly urgent, but something obvious that he had never considered before. His benefactor, Wilton Knight, had cultivated a taste for straight coffee much like Michael's blood father. Wilton Knight, in saving Michael's life, had assumed the role of surrogate father. Knight's doctors took him off coffee shortly before he and Michael met, restricting him to tepid, weak tea, and only two cups per day at maximum.

Shortly thereafter, Wilton Knight had died.

There was no direct causal effect, Michael knew, but the sequence still existed, demanding to be taken into account.

Michael rose, poured himself another slug of the hot, rich coffee, and got down to business.

'You know, Angie, last night I was really nervous about walking into this thing with the Stones. I figured if they'd made my identity we were all goners. But now Roberto has split, and he knows how to find the Stones from our conversation and the setup of the weapons deal. It just occurred to me that now we *have* no choice. We have to make the date if for no other reason than to try to intercede and keep Roberto and a lot of other Langunas and Laguna sympathizers from acquiring a bullet-hole collection.'

'That's why I wish he'd stayed in Gatesville,' said Angie, mostly into her cup. 'He's been making noises about a showdown, a hard line, a once-and-for-all kind of conflict with the Stones.'

'*High Noon* in Houston, huh? Roberto's a real cowboy, alright.'

'You could be driving into the middle of a war,' she said, not liking the idea of riding along on such a death-drive herself.

'Don't worry. Last night I tried to anticipate a few contingencies.' *As Devon would say.* 'No harm in telling you that among other things, my car is bullet-proof – even against the kind of hardware the Stones can scare up. If you stay in the car you'll be reasonably safe.'

The problem was, as Michael saw it, that to perpetrate the arms-deal deception, *he* might have to leave the safety of KITT's cabin.

'Are you going to change your clothes?' he said, dropping that little worry.

'Yes. I wandered in last night and just collapsed. God, I must look like an absolute mess.' She raked her fingers through her hair and headed for the bathroom, avoiding the bureau mirror and the terrors it might hold in store.

Michael rubbed his eyes clear. Angie wasted no time getting ready. By six-thirty they were on the road, headed for Tower Rock Pass.

D.D. bellied down in the gravel and rockfall that littered the V of one of Tower Rock Pass's principal peaks, and socketed binoculars into his eyes.

It was beginning to lighten up, but the infrared Nitefinder lenses did not discriminate between night and day. D.D. was decked out in Marine sandfighting fatigues of light tan, with an engineer's bandanna knotted around his forehead. His bulky Auto Mag was holstered in khaki canvas under his arm, and slung over one shoulder was a bandolier of what looked like fat aluminium bullets – shells for the Malko cartridge launcher on the ground by his feet. His teeth worked a wooden toothpick down to shards and he spat into the dust.

'Gotta vehicle concentration,' he said over his shoulder.

Ricky perched a fully loaded American 180 on his hip. He was similarly dressed. All the Stones were, and all had come out for this little sortie. Sand goggles were pushed up on Ricky's forehead; his web belt was festooned with phosphorus grenades that dangled like deadly olive-drab Christmas tree ornaments.

'Buncha stupid Mexicans with Chevys for jeeps and shotguns for firepower.' Ricky shook his head. 'We're gonna clean their slate and Michael Knight's at the same time.' He hoisted a field walkie-talkie to his head and depressed the talk button. 'Spanky to Buckwheat – how's the rest of Our Gang?'

'Buckwheat yo,' came the response. 'Established as per plan. Crossfire pattern on valley set up; Farina entrenched with rocket launcher at mouth of the valley. Orders? Come back.'

'Orders as follows,' transmitted Ricky to the group. 'Fire signal will be phosphorus, repeat, phosphorus. On positive sight fire at will. Kill everything not wearing a desert suit, repeat – give them total hell. One more thing: If you get positive sighting on a green Firebird, that one's mine. Any man who takes it out before me is subject to my disciplinary actions. Copy?'

Acknowledgements came in from the rest of the Stones positions. Ricky wanted Roberto all to himself.

'Got four, maybe five cars in convoy,' said D.D. from the observation point. 'ETA about five minutes. With luck we'll have the rising sun behind us.'

'Spanky to Rolling Stone,' Ricky continued. 'Report progress.'

Rolling Stone was the backup getaway truck, different from the larger truck in which the Stones had brought their weapons and supplies. Its task was seeding the roadway leading through the belly of Tower Rock Pass with concussion landmines.

'Rolling Stone yo,' came the transmission. 'The snake has fangs. Over.' That indicated that the road – the 'snake' – was alive with mines that had been neatly buried, armed, and concealed from casual notice.

D.D. could see a dust trail kicked up by the oncoming convoy. 'Damned amateurs,' he muttered, and started on another toothpick.

'They had to have been tipped by Michael Knight,' said Ricky. 'Otherwise, they wouldn't have shown up right on time for the buy – they knew what time the buy was set for.

Knight's a double. Working for who, I'm not sure yet. But he goes out this morning along with the rest of them. Besides, we get the bonus of getting to keep his cash, and the pleasure of stringing him along and blowing him away.' He looked at the predawn sky and extended his arms in a cruciform pose, like an Indian worshipping some obscure god of battle. 'Even the sun is with us today,' he said cryptically.

'What about Angie?' said D.D. 'I get the feeling she's swung away from the Stones. If she's hanging out with Michael Knight, then it's logical to assume she's been in contact with the Lagunas.'

'Yeah . . . poor, pretty Angie. It'll be a shame to fill a body like hers up with nothing but holes. Oh well. Fortunes of war.' Ricky seemed absurdly happy on the morn of battle. 'They'll all go to the Happy Hunting Ground at the group rate.'

'Then?'

'Then, *mi amigo*, we haul stakes for Seattle. We've got a boat to catch. Emile Pavlon set up a prime buy-in for us in Hong Kong.'

'Why?'

'As a present for getting him out of Torreon, and giving him some walking cash. It'll take him awhile to get back into the mainstream of smuggling after two years in stir. Meantime, he's referring juicy deals to the Stones with his compliments.'

'Nice,' nodded D.D. 'Maybe Emile is about to make himself obsolete.'

'That's what I was thinking, good buddy,' said Ricky, poison in his voice. 'If Emile doesn't retire *real* soon, he might just *be* retired by us.'

'Sounds solid.' Betrayal and opportunism were standard coinages in which the Stones regularly dealt. If Emile Pavlon was really a professional, he'd smell the new order coming and gracefully step out of the way. D.D. brought Ricky back to the present by adding, 'But first we got a little desert firefight to get out of the way before all these big plans proceed.'

'Gotcha,' said Ricky, picking up the walkie-talkie again. 'Spanky to Our Gang. The fish are on their way into the net. Hunker down and wait for the phosphorus . . . repeat . . . wait for the phosphorus. . . .'

Roberto Laguna braced the M-16 automatic against the heavy, rigid cast on his right arm and worked the action with his left. The mechanism clicked loudly; the first shell was chambered. On rapidfire, with a thirty-round clip, he thought he would be able to hit *something*, even shooting with his left hand. His 'devil's hand,' according to the mythology that dictated southpaws to somehow be in league with the forces of Hell. Carlos would go for that, he thought. Carlos – *Father* Carlos – was all platitudes and no action; he talked the talk but he didn't walk the walk.

Around him, the Lagunas and the Laguna auxiliary had got out of their cars for a final powwow. The men numbered about twenty, with Enrique serving as war-chief, a holdover position from their teenage gang days. Roberto, being blood-Laguna, set the pattern; Enrique implemented the plan.

Roberto saw them all – Alfredo Cruz, Chico Ramirez, all three of the Ruiz brothers, the bulking weightlifting form of Ricardo Esteban Morales, friends, and friends of friends, all shouldering a variety of weapons. Some had 12-gauge automatic shotguns, police riot rifles. Enrique had come up with a small collection of M-16s and enough ammunition to blow away the population of China. The Laguna weapons backstock had been tapped, and so there were a few Nunn Nineteens in the group. They had LAW and SAM-17 rockets and smoke bombs for quick cover. They had grenades and pistols and killing knives and their bare, dedicated hands, and they were waiting for the word.

Roberto felt proud.

He wanted his pride to spill over and infuse his men with courage and the strength of being on the right side. He perched the M-16 on his hip (in exactly the way Ricky was doing, some five miles distant, as he gave his own crew a pep talk), and turned his gaze toward Tower Rock Pass.

'There will be a black car, the same car that interceded at Teresa's wedding reception at the Del Rio. It is not to be harmed. The man driving it has allowed us the information that will today mean the end of the *Corazones de Piedras* and their reign of terror. *Comprende?*'

Each man nodded or voiced their understanding.

'Then we attack at dawn. Chico, you drive my car; I shall ride and fire from the passenger side and the sunroof. Enrique has the truck; it is armoured, as are the other cars. The Stones do not suspect this. They have probably planted explosives. Once we approach the Pass, avoid the road. Enrique and I shall establish a convergence point. That is when you, Ricardo, and you, Chuy, come into play.'

Ricardo and Chuy were piloting heavily shielded off-road vehicles, strange-looking hybrids of tank and dune buggy, with huge, knobby tyres. They did not have to stick to the roadway; they could drive right up the side of the mountain if they had to. The Stones did not know, Roberto felt sure, about their special vehicles, either – they had a habit of underestimating the Lagunas simply because they had got away with killing a few of them.

That would change, Roberto reflected, in about ten minutes.

Feeling somewhat like Pancho Villa, Roberto said simply, 'We ride. *Vamanos!*'

'I'm scared, Michael,' Angie said as KITT barrelled along in the predawn darkness – the time when the night, about to relinquish its claim on the earth, is darkest. 'I have this awful feeling about this whole thing . . . it's going to be okay, isn't it?'

'It'll be okay. Don't get out of the car, that's all.'

'*Michael*,' said KITT. '*I'm getting some very active readings.*'

'How far are we from Tower Rock Pass, KITT?' The digital clock on the Super Dash read 6:51 a.m.

'*Six miles. I'm reading a group of vehicles proceeding along the same road as we are approximately two miles ahead of us. There are from four to six separate engines running. There are*

146

also bulk metallic readings bouncing back from the Pass itself.'

'Roberto . . .' breathed Angie. 'He's called out the Lagunas . . .'

'And the Stones are laying for them up in the hills,' finished Michael. 'I guess we'll never find out if they intended to ambush *me* or not.'

'They'll all be killed!'

'We shouldn't have mentioned the location to Roberto,' said Michael. 'Damn! We should have known he'd jump the gun – even wounded.'

The dust from the column just ahead was flowing around KITT's windows now.

'Additional readings,' reported KITT. *'A large vehicle, possibly a truck, secreted out of sight on ground level. Men on the peaks, most probably armed. The readings I'm registering indicate that the cars ahead are heavily armoured.'*

'Roberto told me that the Firebird was "shielded," once,' remembered Angie. 'I didn't know what he meant at the time. I guess –'

'He meant armoured against penetration from heavy-calibre slugs, most likely,' said Michael. 'The Lagunas aren't as dumb as the Stones think.'

They were all coming up on the Pass. The eastern horizon was beginning to light up.

'Hang onto your fenders, old buddy,' said Michael to KITT. 'Here we go.' And he pushed the pedal down.

14

From the top of Tower Rock Pass, Ricky watched the line of cars push toward the Stones' position. In the smoke and dust he could not see the bulletlike form of KITT moving in fast, bringing up the rear of the Laguna attack line.

D.D. ditched his infrared binoculars and picked up a copy of the Nunn Nineteen machine-gun. He assumed the Laguna cars were armoured; while other members of the Stones were adroit at blowing out tyres, perforating radiators and otherwise crippling vehicles, D.D. hated wasting bullets on metal. He always shot for the windshields, going straight for the occupants, rather than the vehicle itself. His finger tightened on the trigger as the Laguna cars closed in. They were nearly to the mouth of the tiny valley now – five vehicles total, with the green Firebird Ricky had set his sights on second in line.

D.D. did not care for Ricky's directives and authoritative posture. He would shoot at anything he damned well pleased; any available target was fair game. His finger tightened on the trigger of the Nunn Nineteen, and he closed one eye, to sight.

'Wait for it,' said Ricky from behind him.

The cars were yards away from the first land mine.

Ricky jerked the pin from his phosphorus grenade, dropping it to the ground amid cigarette butts and the shredded remains of D.D.'s toothpicks. He got ready to lob it downward.

'Wait for it . . .!'

The armoured offroad truck driven by Enrique, one of the veterans of the attack by the Stones on the wedding reception, rolled over the trip for the first string of mines at nearly fifty miles an hour. A blinding detonation coughed up from the road, splitting it in two and pitching the truck into the air at the same speed.

Enrique screamed as the truck lifted off. The plating on the chassis kept deadly shrapnel from the mine from ripping him to shreds from below, but the truck in which he and two others of the Laguna fighting force were riding was now flipping end-over-end, out of control. Bilious black smoke rolled skyward from the jagged ditch dug out by the explosion.

The truck touched down on its right side and slid. On impact, one of the guns packed into the cab went off, blowing out the rear windshield. The passengerside door was staved in by the force of landing, but the heavy rollbar kept the cab from imploding like tinfoil.

Enrique saw one of his own wheels roll past, on fire.

Grabbing an M-16, he struggled to punch his way out of the wreckage.

Roberto watched Enrique's truck fly into the air as though from a daredevil's jump-ramp. It spun around and smashed into the ground, spraying parts and fire. Chico stood on the brakes of the Firebird and it smoked to a stop scant feet in front of the explosion trench.

Behind them, the dune-buggy vehicles peeled off to the left and right, avoiding the road.

'This is it!' he shouted. 'We fight from here!'

He leaned out the window and fired his M-16, left-handed, at the hillside.

He saw Enrique poke his head out of the demolished truck about twenty yards ahead, and then, between Roberto and the truck, a phosphorus grenade went off with a noisy, *crumping* burst of blinding chemical fire.

Traces of sizzling phosphorus arced through the air in a peculiar, shimmering spiderweb pattern, igniting whatever they touched on the ground. Scrub bushes and tumbleweeds began to burn with a mesquite smell.

Roberto continued firing, even though he could not see a damned thing, including the arrival of KITT, right behind him.

When Ricky's grenade touched off the Stones opened fire with everything they could muster.

D.D. gleefully peppered the truck that had run over the mine with weapons fire, blowing in the front windshield and causing the occupants inside to twitch, jerk, scream, and die. One of them managed to jump out and get to cover behind the truck, which was laying on its side like a dead buffalo. D.D. continued firing, aiming for the gas tank. He wanted to get that last man.

Ricky and several other Stones began letting the Firebird have it. The windshield and tyres exploded as the driver and passenger dived for cover behind the open doors, brandishing weapons.

At about eight o'clock from Ricky's position, the Stone known on the radio as Farina – actually an Ex-Green Beret named Nick Ronson (who joked about his name because in Viet Nam he had handled napalm) – cut loose with a LAW rocket. The bazookalike shell left a smoke trail as it flew across the mouth of the pass and picked off one of the dune buggies, making it an airborne fireball. The driver and shotgun rider bailed out – one of them in flames – and the buggy made a mess of itself on the rock formations at the base of the hill.

Ricky saw Ronson's arms swan out as M-16 fire stitched a line of holes in him running from his left hip to his right shoulder. He fell down and stayed down.

151

'Cover that other buggy!' Ricky screamed, but the buggy was already raising hell on the other side of the pass. Something came apart with a violent explosion, causing a miniature avalanche of rocks, dead Stones, and their weapons, and sending an orange fireball billowing up like a miniature rising sun.

Slugs keened off the desert rocks inches from Ricky and D.D.'s heads. They returned fire, Ricky using the American 180 until he realized the clouds of dust and the smoke from the explosions were fouling the laser sights. He tossed the expensive weapon to the ground and slotted himself behind a .50-calibre machine gun set up on a tripod near D.D.

The racket of the automatic weapons fire all around them was incredible. Ricky wished he could whistle up some helicopter support, like in the good old days.

D.D. turned his attention from the crippled truck to the trapped Firebird. The fighting had been going on for perhaps seven seconds since the mine explosion, but time always seemed to elongate in battle. D.D. changed clips, fast and effortlessly, then took care of the Firebird, blowing away the driver when he peeked out to fire. The man flipped over backwards and sprawled in the dirt.

Ricky was about to open up on the Firebird himself when he saw KITT, coming on at full speed.

Michael and Angie had almost caught up with the Laguna column when Enrique's truck was taken out by the mine. It took the first few crucial seconds of the battle for KITT to close the gap, running at close to ninety miles an hour on the unrefined road.

All Angie could see were explosions all around, and the green Firebird screeching to a halt, and Roberto jumping out with an automatic rifle.

'You were right about the mines, KITT!' Michael shouted.

They were not slowing down as the rear end of the Firebird drew closer at high speed. The dune buggies had already veered off, headed for the hills.

'Hang on!' said Michael. There was no time for seat belts.

Angie grabbed the armrests.

When a crash into the firebird looked unavoidable, Michael punched the TURBO BOOST button.

With a jolting whoosh of air compression, KITT lifted off and cleared the Firebird by ten vertical feet. Angie screamed.

KITT's supershocks absorbed much of the landing impact, but not Angie's immediate terror. 'How the hell did you do that?' she gasped.

'It's one of the factory options,' said Michael. 'Hang tight!'

Another mine blew the road apart underneath KITT, actually lifting the car into the air again for a brief instant. Rocks, dirt, pavement, and shrapnel flew around but KITT was not impeded.

'They're all up in the peaks,' said Michael. 'Cut loose the MR-90, KITT. Do a hard U-turn at the other end of the pass – we'll seesaw until we exhaust the tank!' Michael lost his grip of the wheel as another mine exploded under them. KITT rolled on.

'*As you wish, Michael,*' KITT replied.

Thick green smoke, like dyed cotton batting, began to spume out from KITT's emitters, mounted to the left and right of the exhausts. It filled up the belly of the pass amazingly fast, making it look like a fantasyland with a green, smoky sea.

Michael stomped on the brakes, executing a speed turn. They slid over a mine, which blew up, but the shrapnel pattered harmlessly off KITT's smooth alloy hide.

Bullets were richocheting off the hood and windshields from many directions now, leaving spark trails and striking up a miniature light show. Angie had the fleeting impression that this was what the interior of a lightning cloud must look like . . . only this cloud was forest green in colour. Heavier slugs raked across the car, making pounding noises on the outside. Not rain, she thought. It was more like a deadly hailstorm, heard from the inside of the car. Miraculously, not a single shell had penetrated to harm her or Michael.

KITT reached the end of Tower Rock Pass. Michael twisted the wheel, slewing the car sideways and spinning its nose around so they faced back the way they had just come.

Michael punched buttons in a hurry. 'On AUTO, KITT,' he said. 'Visibility is zero.'

On sensors alone they ploughed back through the fog of the dispersing MR-90 gas, laying down another layer of the stuff. Weapons fire directed at the black car had already diminished.

'You can't hit what you can't see,' Michael said triumphantly.

'What about Roberto?' Angie insisted. 'What does this gas do?'

'Don't worry – it'll just make everybody cry so much they won't be able to shoot, then it'll make them nice and sleepy.'

'What the hell do we do with a bunch of sleeping mercenaries?'

'Devon's probably alerted the authorities now . . . now that we've got something somebody can be arrested for. Now the Stones don't even need that truckload of American 180s and Nunn Nineteens to be locked up for a few decades – this firefight is all the excuse anyone will need to put them away.'

'I thought I saw Chico get hit on the first pass,' said Angie, concerned more now about stray shots hitting her lover in the fog than by any bullets flying in her direction. KITT was a safe vantage point from which to watch the whole noisy action.

'We'll be able to check on Roberto in a second,' Michael said, not really sure.

'The Firebird is dead ahead,' said KITT. *'I detect bodies, but no living persons in its immediate vicinity.'*

When the thick green gas filled up the valley and began to rise invitingly toward the Stones' position in the jagged vee of the Tower Rock peak, Ricky gave up trying to hit the black car with the .50-calibre.

D.D. was watching the gas rise. 'What the hell is that!'

He had watched, somewhat awed, as all the Stones had unleashed their firepower on the black car . . . and still it had completed its run to the end of the Pass. Not only that, it had turned around and come hurling back for more. Clearly the car was some kind of ordnance they had not anticipated, had never heard of, and perhaps could not comprehend.

Scared by the inability of their weapons to stop the car, D.D. hid his feelings by lashing out at Ricky in anger: 'This is *your* fault, dammit! We shoulda scragged that Knight guy back in the hotel room – or before then, at the ranch!'

'His presence here is no accident,' said Ricky. 'Perhaps I misread his significance . . .'

D.D. knew that Ricky was again speaking of his strange, mystic visions and his bent for Indian lore. He ignored it. 'Look!' he shouted, pointing across the valley to what they could still see of the Stones' entrenchment amid the green, swirling vapour.

The Stones were coughing, sputtering, letting their weapons drop.

Down on the ground, the Lagunas were doing likewise. The remaining attack buggy rolled wildly out of control and jacked itself up against a rockpile, where it stayed with its front wheel ludicrously spinning around and around while the occupants lost their weapons and fought for air, weeping.

The blood drained from Ricky's face. He slid his goggles on, but sensed that would do little good.

'Some kinda riot gas!' said D.D. They both knew that the Stones had brought along no CBW masking gear this trip. They were as vulnerable to gas attack as a blind snake is to a hungry hawk.

Ricky grabbed D.D.'s arm and pulled his sweating face inches from his own. D.D.'s bandanna was nearly touching the goggles. 'The truck – Rolling Stone,' he hissed. 'Let's get the hell out of here!'

'What about the men?'

'Remember what we used to say in 'Nam,' Ricky said, with a gesture like a shrug. The gas would flood their position in five more seconds, then *all* the Stones would be incapacitated.

'Yeah – cover your butt and to hell with the hindmost,' said D.D.

'Right on.' He jerked D.D. away from the position and snatched up the American 180 from the ground. Together the two *Corazones de Piedras* made fast, fleeing-coyote tracks for the concealed getaway truck.

The MR-90 worked like a wizard's curse.

The fighting forces forgot about their weapons, needing their hands to rub their eyes and grope around. In this condition, the Stones and Lagunas could not even tell each other apart.

'*A most efficacious deterrent to fighting,*' noted KITT.

'Yeah,' said Michael. 'No wonder the government didn't want to develop it. It would have put too many war industries out of business.'

KITT slid to a stop a few feet away from the Firebird. There were a few feet of visibility now; Michael could see Chico thrashing around on the ground next to the driver's side door. Blood was pumping out of a wound in his shoulder, and the effects of the gas were causing him no small amount of pain as he tossed and twisted, trying to shake off the temporary damage to his nose and eyes. The gas made your own glands render you harmless.

Roberto was nowhere to be seen.

In the hazy, greened-over distance, Enrique staggered away from the flaming wreckage of his truck, which had finally been ignited by D.D.'s machine gun. His face was glistening with tears and his hands were clamped over his ears. He tripped over a jut of stone and tumbled to the ground. Oily smoke curled upward from the burning truck, and the air now smelled like scorching rubber.

The only other injury that occurred after Michael had dispersed the gas was to another Stone, an ex-Ranger named Harlan Trumball. Blinded, eyes watering from the gas, he dropped his machine gun and walked straight off the cliff edge of the pass, falling some thirty feet and breaking his right leg in two places.

'KITT, any readings that might indicate where Roberto made off to?'

Angie was already sobbing and looking about nervously, having assumed the worst.

'No, Michael. Although my radio surveillance indicates that Devon has dispatched county sheriffs to the area. They should be arriving in the next five minutes. Shall I order up some paramedic units, as well?'

'Good idea, buddy,' he said. 'Now, if only we could somehow find –'

'Roberto!!' Angie yelped.

Before Michael could stop her she shoved open the car door and was running.

'Angie, no –!'

He followed her line of sight and saw Roberto slumped against the west wall of the valley, inside the curve of the cliffside. But Angie had opened the door and jumped free of the car, and the gas had not totally blended with the air yet, to degrade to harmless residue.

Some of the potent air wafted into the car as Angie fled to the aid of her lover. There was no time for analysis. 'KITT! Shut the door! Blowers on full!'

'Oh, my goodness,' said KITT, complying instantaneously. *'That young woman apparently has no regard for her own safety. The gas would have rinsed away into the air in another four-point-two minutes . . . Michael, are you affected?'*

The sensation was astounding. A second after KITT automatically slammed Angie's door, Michael's eyes welled up with dense tears. His sinuses and mucus membranes seemed to inflate with moisture and his skin tingled unnaturally. In another second, he was totally incapacitated, hot saline tears streaming freely from his eyes.

'KITT,' he said in a choked, dry voice. The gas had locked up his throat as well. 'Did Angie make it over to Roberto?'

'They both seem to be clutching each other . . . crying,' KITT said coolly.

'He's alive, then.'

'He seems to be.'

Michael wiped tears away with both hands, but it did no good. His eyes were tearing twice as fast as he could mop at his face.

'*There are no traces of the gas left in the cabin, Michael. Do you feel better yet?*'

'There are plenty of traces of the gas left in my system,' he growled, 'and that's what counts. God, is this stuff ever potent.'

'*Michael – I'm registering a truck engine turning over. Readings indicate the presence of weapons in the truck bed. It looks like all the Stones may not have been incapacitated by the MR-90.*'

'Terrific; I can't see a damned thing except blurry outlines and I feel like my head is inside a fishbowl.'

'*They're heading out of the pass at high speed. Should we pursue them or wait until you are fully functional?*'

'Dumb question,' gasped Michael. 'Go. Go on AUTO PURSUIT; let's go get them.'

KITT's gears engaged without Michael's help; the PURSUIT bar blinked blue, and the car backed up and turned around by itself while its driver wheezed and pawed at his leaking eyes.

'I hope I can see by the time we catch up with them,' Michael said ruefully.

KITT's red digital speedometer flew past fifty, then seventy-five as the black car sped out of Tower Rock Pass.

15

'See anything behind us?' Ricky said as he goosed the speedometer of the truck past eighty on the crudely hewn back road.

D.D. stared through the cab's large camper window, out through the open camper bay. The bed of the truck was heavy with crated weapons, Nunn Nineteens and American 180s. 'Nothing!' he shouted back. 'No pursuit that I can see.'

'In forty-five minutes we'll be in Mexico,' Ricky said. 'I've got a border-jump contingency set up already . . . just in case something like this happened.'

'You mean we're driving straight through with a truckload of guns?'

'You got it. It took a lot of grease, but the boys on the border checkpoint are all well-compensated *compadres*.'

D.D. laughed, expelling tension. 'That's the first good news I've heard all day.'

'We'll take a week or two and do what any efficient combat unit does,' continued Ricky. 'Regroup. We've got the petty cash fund we used to spring Emile Pavlon; we'll just lay low with some *señoritas* and some good tequila for a week or so . . . and then we'll come back across and kick the stuffing out of Michael Knight.'

'We may not have to wait,' D.D. said, pointing. 'He's right behind us!'

Ricky shot a glance into the review mirror and saw that it was true. 'Where did he *come* from –?'

'Don't ask me. What we gotta do is shake him off our tail.'

Ricky kept one hand on the wheel and grabbed a Nunn Nineteen with the other. 'I got a great way to do that.'

D.D. clambered through the camper window and aimed his own weapon out the back of the truck. After a second to check his loads, he began firing on KITT with one of the bulky Malko cartridge launchers.

'*How are your eyes, Michael?*' said KITT.

'Better. I can see shapes but not details.' His face was wet, and the tailgate of the truck bearing Ricky and D.D. away was perhaps a hundred yards distant.

'*A fortunate thing that you only got a small taste of the MR-90. . . .*'

'Believe me, KITT – that's all the taste I *ever* want to get!'

A sudden explosion rocked the car, causing KITT to veer swiftly to port.

'*What was that?*' said KITT.

'Don't ask me,' returned Michael. 'I still can't see a thing.'

The first charge was followed by several more as the plump little Malko cartridges homed in and blew up like miniature missiles. Subsequent charges threw up smoke and phosphorus. It was quite a spectacular barrage.

'*Michael, I don't like this. Those charges are large enough to give me surface dents!*'

'Bonnie'll fix you up. Just catch them!'

'*How do you propose to stop them?*' Another explosion weaved them to the right.

'Go to MANUAL,' said Michael. 'I think I can see now.'

'*Are you sure?*' KITT didn't like bravery when his own chassis was concerned.

'Do it! That looks like D.D. in –' another shot landed in front of them, detonating and washing the hood briefly with grey smoke, making Michael flinch. 'That looks like D.D. in the back of the truck, giving us hell. Satisfied? Now go to MANUAL!'

KITT complied and Michael took the wheel. His eyes stung and smarted, but he could make out the chase truck, when a few moments before everything had been a colourless blur, like black and white TV static.

Up ahead, D.D. paused to reload. Michael poured on the speed, closing the gap between the two vehicles. D.D. looked up, saw him coming, dropped the cartridge launcher and began to strafe KITT's front end with machinegun fire. Yellow sparks scratched hotly off the alloy, flying backward.

Michael punched in the TURBO BOOST function again.

D.D. must have divined what was about to happen, for panic washed over his face in the instant Michael depressed the firing button. He threw his Nunn Nineteen aside and lept pell-mell out of the truck bed, taking his chances and perhaps saving his life (at the cost of his skin) as KITT became airborne.

The gleaming black nose ripped into the camper shell where D.D. had stood a second before, splitting it wide and wedging into the truck bed with a crash that caused both the rear tyres to disintegrate. Cases of crated rifles somersaulted through the air and burst open on contact with the arid desert hardpack. The rear bumper met the ground and dug a wide ditch describing the path of the crippled truck as it whipped insanely about, speed diminishing. An enormous cloud trail of dusty smoke rose in the truck's wake as the bed dug into the dirt.

With the disproportionate weight of KITT in the back, the truck began to skid sideways, coughing up even more dust and desert sand. They were now inside a tornado of flying brown grit.

'Reverse thrust!' yelled Michael. 'Get us back on the ground!'

KITT rocketed himself off the truck bed, the pressure of

takeoff breaking the truck chassis in half. The whole crippled mess catapulted to a stop as KITT hit the ground, wheels turning, kicking up even more suffocating dust.

Ricky's attempts to keep the truck's steering wheel stable had failed. The truck was a goner. He grabbed up his own machine gun and jumped free of the wreck just as KITT pulled up alongside.

Michael did not wait for KITT to stop to pile out of the driver's seat. Squinting heavily, he ran around to where Ricky was trying to haul his weapon up into the firing line and loaded his fist into the mercenary's mouth.

The gun flew away. Ricky blocked Michael's next punch and countered with one to his stomach. Michael saw it coming but could not get out of the way; his eyes were not doing their part and he could barely see. The air huffed out of him as Ricky's fist sank in. He *did* see the kick that came next, and caught Ricky's boot in his hands, twisting it and kicking out himself.

Ricky did an involuntary pirouette in the air, banging his skull against the front fender of the truck. Michael scrambled over and was on top of him in an instant.

'Here's one for your third Indian eye,' Michael said, and gave Ricky everything he had, packed into his right fist and delivered solidly to the target point of Ricky's broad nose.

Ricky's eyes rolled up to pure whites, like window-shades, and he collapsed down into dreamland.

About two hundred yards back, D.D. was clawing at his leg and wailing for help. The jump from the truck at high speed had netted him a broken leg much like Harlan Trumball's, and he was at least fifty yards from the nearest of the spilled weapons. Even his automatic Magnum had dropped from its holster, and was now lost in the dust . . . somewhere, for some scrounger to discover it long after it had rusted to uselessness.

The woop-woop clanger of a police siren cut through the still desert air. Michael climbed back into KITT to wait.

'I guess I'll see what all this looks like in tomorrow's newspaper,' he lamented, still crying.

The mop-up proved to be much neater than the firefight had been. Devon arrived on the heels of the authorities, riding in the back of an unmarked government-issue sedan. KITT and Michael drove back to Tower Rock Pass once several deputy sheriffs showed up to collect Ricky and D.D. and keep an eye on the American 180s and Nunn Nineteens that were scattered everywhere. Weapons littered the perimeter of the truck like deadly, high-tech fallout.

Michael found Angie and Roberto near the demolished green Firebird. Roberto was sitting on the hood. The front end of the car had sagged toward the ground, its wheels shot out from under. Angie helped her lover dab at his face with a damp cloth. All around, police and sheriff's deputies collected guns, and pieces of guns, loading everything into a panel truck that looked like it had been diverted from SWAT duty.

Devon put his hand on Michael's shoulder. His positive, paternal air had returned. 'Things seem to have worked out quite nicely, my boy,' he said, beaming.

Around them, junked autos smouldered and burned. The black hash marks of explosions were everywhere, circled by debris, and paramedics were filling up ambulances with the wounded. It seemed queerly like Devon was pleased with all the destruction.

'Yeah,' said Michael. 'Only ten or twelve people got killed or maimed. Not bad. All in a day's work.'

The hand stayed on his shoulder. 'Michael – you saved quite a few lives today. When you have a bunch of insane, determined people with sophisticated guns . . . many, many more could have died. It's not right that even one had to . . . even one Stone. We both know how the cards tend to fall in a deal like this.'

'So now the *Corazones de Piedras* are signed, sealed, and delivered. So now the Lagunas can go on doing virtually what the Stones were doing in the first place . . . only with the sanction of the government, right?'

'It's not the same,' Devon said, walking Michael to the truck. 'Knight Industries is no longer involved. My conscience is clear – as yours should be – about our

163

participation in the construction of those weapons. We *did* catch the Stones "hot", and we *did* arrest a shipment of American 180s and Nunn Nineteens. A huge shipment. We're out of it now.'

'That seems the best,' Michael agreed. 'It just leaves a rotten taste, that's all.'

'What's the story with Angie and Roberto Laguna?' The pair were still at Roberto's car, but it was clear that the officers standing nearby were waiting for Roberto's eyes to clear up so he could be loaded into a cruiser and booked along with everyone else arrested that afternoon.

'They were on opposite sides of the fence in the war between the Langunas and the Stones,' said Michael. 'In love nevertheless. Their relationship may be the only healthy thing to come out of this – if it lasts. It's been going on behind everybody's backs for a year now.'

'Seems like a fiercely strong commitment,' Devon noted. 'Perhaps I should persuade the authorities to make an exception in Roberto's case. Would you advise it?'

Michael stopped in his tracks, looking at Devon in his business suit, with his precisely groomed hair and open expression. 'Are you asking *my* advice?' he said, cocking a thumb at himself in disbelief.

Devon said nothing; he smiled enigmatically.

'Sure, why not?' said Michael. 'Why disrupt the course of true love?' He felt better, lighter, already.

'You do still have the money, don't you?' Devon added, in the same calm tone, and that made Michael laugh a bit.

'The bottom line,' he said, peering up into the hot desert sky. 'KITT's got the briefcase. We never even got around to faking the weapons buy – it was useful, though.' He was thinking of the scene at the Shanghai Inn, where he had used the money to convince the Stones he was a bona fide buyer . . . right before Emile Pavlon breezed in and blew Michael's cover. 'What about Pavlon?' he added. 'Did you pick him up?'

In the distance, Michael saw Roberto giving him the thumbs-up, the high sign, a big slaphappy grin daubed across his face. Michael gave the couple a half-hearted little wave of acknowledgement, feeling slightly sick about the circumstances.

'Pavlon left the country as soon as he could,' said Devon. 'No reports.'

'Win some, lose some fish,' said Michael. 'How about the Lagunas? Business as usual?'

'You and I could go visit Father Carlos and find out,' the silver-haired Knight Industries version of Merlin replied.

Michael chewed on that for a moment. 'No. I don't want to deal with Father Carlos's doubletalk again or I might lose this great mood I'm cultivating.'

Hands clasped rearward as they walked, Devon nodded in bitter understanding.

Michael watched the activity a bit longer, lingering, then turned back to Devon. 'Need a lift into town?'

Devon sniffed. 'You don't expect me to hoof it back, do you?'

'I see you're absorbing some of the local vernacular. You'll be a redneck in no time.'

'Hm, quite. All I need do now is learn what the –' he paused to get it right '– the "Texas Two-Step" is.'

They got into the waiting form of the Knight Industries Two Thousand and drove back to Houston.

'Bonnie! Ay que chula!'

Bonnie coloured. 'Why, thank you, KITT.' She was waiting for Michael and Devon in the office portion of the service truck. To Michael's amazement she was dressed not in her characteristic jumper – her second skin – but in a light, smooth dress the colour of a fresh peach. It contrasted with her even skin tone quite distractingly. There was a scalloped ruffle running along the plunging neckline, and a tiny golden belt with spangles. The dress showed off her legs, in nylons and heels. It was the first time Michael had ever seen Bonnie Barstow's legs.

He thought he was dreaming. 'Show-off,' he muttered to the car.

He had showered, shaved and dressed for the evening, and felt substantially more human. KITT had been washed and vacuumed and was glittering. Michael sat in the pilot seat while the ramp lowered itself.

'Well,' he said with a touch of regret. 'You and Devon have fun tonight, Bonnie.' And he backed KITT out quickly, a mischievous smile on his face.

'Hey, wait a minute!' said Bonnie, chasing him out, moving on her heels not clumsily at all. It was hard to run down the truck's corrugated steel ramp gracefully . . . but she did it, and caught up with him just as Devon pulled his Bentley around into the Houston Plaza lot to meet them.

Her hands locked on the open-window portion of KITT's door. 'Where do you think you're going, Mr Knight? You owe me a steak.'

'Medium rare,' Michael smiled. 'But not tonight, love. I've got a date with a nurse named Barry.'

'*Barry?*' she said, goggling. 'But why . . . I mean . . . uh – what about you and me?'

His smile became a gremlin's grin. 'Hang in there, Juliet,' he said recalling their similar exchange of two days ago. 'You might get lucky.'

She stood there flustered, beautiful, her dress wafting around in the light evening breeze. It was fresh off the desert, and solidly warm.

He tooled out of the lot while she watched after him. The balance had been restored. From this stage they might go anywhere.

While waiting at the light near the Plaza turn-in, KITT put in: '*Michael, perhaps I should not bring this up, but there is a large, heavy vehicle closing in on us from behind.*'

Michael whipped his head around, anticipating some kind of sneak attack from a Stones auxiliary unit. 'Oh, *no*,' he murmured as the huge, imposing vehicle pulled alongside.

It was the hyperthyroidal Cowboy Cadillac he had encountered before on the streets of Houston. Its row of blazing chrome pipes blatted sparks and exhaust toward his face, and above him the lunatic truck jockey leaned out of his cab.

'*Hey boy!*' the driver screamed, spit flying from his lips.

'Didn't I tell ya to keep that four-wheeled Dee-troit junkpile offa my personal *streets*?' He brayed laughter past the tittering carhop seated in the cab with him.

Michael's face broke apart into a helpless little grin. 'Put your money were your mouth is, ace!' he yelled back.

'Alright! Alright, *Alright!*' the mad trucker bellowed. 'Let's do it to it! On the green, you stand on it, you hear! You're gonna gobble mah dust, you pore youngster – !' The feathers in the guy's crazed cowboy hat flew around as he yelled everything.

'KITT, when that light goes to green, I want all the speed you've ever imagined. We're going to shut this good old boy down.'

'Michael, I'm not quite sure what that means . . .'

'Don't worry about it. Just poor on the speed.'

The truck next door revved again, spewing petro-chemical smoke and fumes, consuming gallons of gas by just idling.

In his mirror, Michael saw Devon link arms with Bonnie in a courtly gesture and escort her to the Bentley.

The light turned green, and from Michael's left there came a roar of acceleration. KITT's speedometer jumped into the double digits, racing toward the hundred mark. In three seconds flat he angled around the truck and put a lot of real estate between them.

High in his cab, the truck jockey whistled in amazement. The last sight he had of KITT was of the black car streaking like a bullet into the glorious Houston sunset.

ABOUT THE AUTHOR

Among ROGER HILL's varied pursuits is the calling of film historian, leading him to make the statement that he 'was made the same year as John Huston's *The African Queen*.' Born in Fort Worth, Texas, and educated at the University of Iowa, Hill has worked as a journalist for major daily newspapers in Las Vegas, Seattle, and Chicago. Since 1977 he has made his home in Studio City, California, and his other interests include music criticism, cartooning, photography, raising Alsatian show dogs, and 'hunting for decent Indonesian food.' This is his sixth novel.